THE BALLAD OF JESSIE PEARL

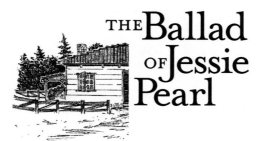

THE Ballad OF Jessie Pearl

Shannon Hitchcock

namelos
South Hampton, New Hampshire

Library of Congress Control Number: 2012936706

ISBN 978-1-60898-141-0 (hardcover : alk. paper)
ISBN 978-1-60898-142-7 (pbk. : alk. paper)
ISBN 978-1-60898-143-4 (ebk.)

namelos
www.namelos.com

For Alex because I promised,
and in memory of Anna, Crawley, and Lena Hennings

 | 1922 |

1 | PUSH

Sometimes when the kerosene lamp casts shadows, I think I see Ma's ghost. If she were still alive, she'd say, *Jessie Pearl, you keep on studying. Not everybody is cut out to be a farm wife. We'll find a way to pay for teachers' college. Leave your pa to me.*

And tonight, Ma would notice how my hands are trembling. I can almost hear her voice. *Jessie, fourteen is too young to help birth a baby. Why don't you go and study in the kitchen?* But Ma is just a memory.

I push Carrie's bobbed hair out of her eyes and smooth it behind her ears. "Don't be afraid, Carrie. Just breathe. Frank's gone for the doctor."

She rocks back and forth on the bed, clutching her enormous belly. "Jessie, get some proper clothes on." Then a pain grips her, and she screams loud enough to wake the animals in the barn.

When the contraction ends, I sprint back to my room. I jerk off my nightclothes and pull on a flannel shirt and overalls. On the way to Pa's room, I twist my hair into one long braid. "Pa," I yell, "Carrie's in labor."

"I heard you," he calls. "Go help your sister. I'll wind some water from the well and get it to boiling."

Carrie screams like a wild animal. I want to tell Pa that I'll wind the water and he can see to Carrie. For the hundredth time today, I wish my ma were here.

"Hurts, back hurts so bad!" Carrie cries. "Pain's tearing me apart."

I climb in bed behind her and rub her back. I rub her legs and feet too. "Good, good girl. It won't be long now. I can't wait to see my new niece."

Carrie shakes her head. "Not a niece. A baby boy."

Pa brings in a basin of hot water and an old sheet torn into rags. I wet one and hold it against Carrie's aching back. "That's...good," she pants.

The pains come in waves. Helplessly, I watch them bubble up, come to a full rolling boil, and finally ebb away. I grip Carrie's hand through each one.

Nearly an hour passes before I hear the chug of Frank's Model T. "He's back, Carrie. Doc will be here in just a minute."

Doors slam and Frank hurries inside with a woman wearing a high-necked black dress and a bonnet.

"Where's the doctor?" I ask.

Frank hurries to Carrie's side and takes her hand. "Little Bobby Pilcher's appendix ruptured. Doc's operatin', so I brought the granny woman instead."

Maude Patterson looks more like a witch than a granny woman. I know Carrie wants a doctor, but beggars don't get to choose.

"Out of here," Maude tells Frank. "The birthin' room ain't no place for a man. Make yourself useful and kill a chicken."

Frank looks at Maude like she's done lost her mind. She waves her arms and swats him out of the room like a fly. "Cook up a pot of chicken soup," she says. "It'll be good for her once the baby's out."

Maude opens up her old satchel. She finds a pair of scissors and slides them under the bed. "That's to cut the pain," she tells me. Next she unfolds a square of gauze. She sprinkles dried herbs inside and ties it up with twine. "Put this in a cup and pour some boiling water over it to steep."

I hold the bag up in front of my face and peer through the gauze. "What's in there?"

"Bethroot, partridgeberry, and blue cohosh," she cackles. "It'll make the pains quicker and stronger."

"Carrie won't be able to stand it if the pains get any stronger," I say. Maude stares at me with her beady eyes. I shut my mouth and make the tea.

We prop Carrie up between us and walk her around the room. "Just let me rest," she moans.

"Walk!" Maude bellows.

The black night fades away, and I turn down the lamp's wick. While I stare out the window at a cold, gray morning, Maude helps Carrie back to bed. She puts her head on Carrie's stomach and listens. "Bring me some lard in a shallow bowl," she says.

I rush to do Maude's bidding, then watch as she greases her arms up to the elbows. I move beside Carrie's head and take her hand. "Push!" Maude yells. "Harder, girl, harder!"

Carrie's face scrunches into a tight knot. She turns bright red, grunts like a pig, and then collapses.

"Not good enough," Maude roars. "You," she says, pointing at me, "get down here and press on her belly."

Tears fill my eyes, and I wipe them on my sleeve. "No! No, ma'am, I'm afraid I'll hurt her."

Maude yanks my arm. "No time to argue. Do it now!"

I press and Carrie pushes. Maude's hands disappear under Carrie's shift again. "The head's out!" Maude shouts. "Help me get her on her hands and knees. The baby's arm is up by its neck, blockin' the shoulders."

That sounds awful. I haul Carrie around like a sack of potatoes.

When the baby slides out into Maude's hands, my stomach seizes. The room goes fuzzy. I grip the iron bed frame, afraid I'm about to be sick.

I don't remember another thing until Maude waves some foul-smelling concoction under my nose. She laughs. "You missed the cord cuttin' and the stitchin' up." She slaps her thigh and says to Carrie, "I don't think this one is meant to be a midwife."

I look up at the old witch as she moves over to her satchel and takes out a black book. "I keep a record of every birth," she says.

Carrie holds the baby boy to her breast. "Look, Jessie. Isn't he beautiful? It's the son I always wanted. The one I promised Frank when he came home from the Great War." She croons a lullaby, sounding just like an angel. "*Hush, little baby, don't you cry.*"

I grab hold of the iron bed and scramble to my feet. My legs are as wobbly as a newborn foal. "I am never having a baby," I tell the old witch. "Be sure and write that down in your black book."

2 | THE MORNING AFTER

"Frank! She did it! She did it! Carrie had a boy!"

Frank leans the pitchfork against the stable and smiles from ear to ear. "How about finishin' up the mornin' chores? I can hardly wait to meet my son."

"Sure, I'll finish up. And take that granny woman home. I think she's a witch."

Frank laughs and runs off toward the house. I'm glad he's better now. He had night terrors after the war. I pitch some hay to Patience, and she makes a whinny that turns into a hee-haw. Mules are awful noisy.

I finish up in the barn and head toward the pigpen. "Pa. Hey, Pa! Carrie had a baby boy!"

He pours a bucket of slop in the trough. "That's mighty good news, Jessie. The house has been too quiet since your ma died."

I hook my arm through his and lean against his side. We watch the pigs shove against each other, trying to be first at the trough. "Maybe the house is too quiet because you're hard of hearing."

Pa chuckles. "Babies do a heap of cryin'. I'll be restin' peaceful while the rest of you can't sleep for the noise."

I hold Ma's faded apron to my face, breathing in the smell of her. She always wore it when she made the biscuits. I collect flour, buttermilk, and lard, then dump some of each into a bowl.

"How's breakfast comin' along?" Pa asks. He sets a gallon bucket of fresh milk on the counter.

"Just fine," I say, which is a big fat lie. Dough is sticking to my hands like glue. Finally I give up and throw the whole mess into a greased skillet. Instead of rolling it into biscuits, I'll bake it whole, like a cake.

Once the bread is in the oven, I dip my hand into a bucket and fling water onto the stovetop. When the droplets dance across, I know it's ready for cooking. I crack eggs into a frying pan and fish out the shells, or most of them. A little crunch never hurt anybody.

"Come and get it," I yell.

Carrie is frowning when I push the door open. "What's wrong?" I ask.

Her frown turns into a gentle smile. "I'm fine, but I'm having trouble breastfeeding. Maybe you could walk down to Anna's and ask her to come for a visit. I could use some sisterly advice."

I place Carrie's breakfast on her bedside table. "Sure, I'll fetch Anna." My sisters are always whispering about husbands and babies, stuff that leaves me out. "So you named him after Pa," I say. "Hezekiah is a big name for such a little fellow."

Carrie nods. "That's why we're calling him Ky." She takes a bite of eggs. "Tastes good, but I don't have much of an appetite."

"You should eat," I say. "Keep up your strength." But then another thought hits me. "Did I ruin the eggs?"

Carrie laughs. "They're good but a little crunchy. Frank brought me some soup earlier."

I walk over to the cradle and poke my finger against Ky's tiny hand. When he closes his fist around it, my heart swells full enough to bust. I pick him up and nuzzle against his soft black hair. "I love him already."

Carrie smiles at me. "I knew you'd love him. You love everybody, except for Liza Phillips."

I nod. "That's because she's stuck on herself."

Carrie raises her eyebrows. "I don't think that's the problem. I think it's because both of you are sweet on J.T."

I put Ky back in his cradle and stick my tongue out at her. "Quit teasing me."

On the way to Anna's, I stop and whistle for Patches. He comes running and knocks me off my feet. I roll with him on the frozen ground. My dog is better company than most people.

He scrambles away and brings back a stick. I throw it toward the dirt road. "Come on, boy. Let's see how fast we can run a mile."

There are no neighbors on the way to Anna and Cole's farm, just plowed fields and deep woods. Cole inherited a lumber company from his daddy, and they're pretty well off compared to most people I know. Racing around to the back porch, I let myself into the kitchen.

"Jessie," Anna scolds, "where are your mittens?"

I blow on my reddened hands. "I forgot about them in all the excitement. Carrie had a baby boy early this morning."

Anna gasps. "Tell me every single detail."

I sit down at the oak table and take a deep sniff. "Is that cinnamon toast?"

Anna nods her head and smiles. "Have you had breakfast?"

"Yes, but I'm still hungry."

After Anna pours coffee, I tell her about Carrie's labor, the granny woman, and Ky's birth. The only part I leave out is how I fainted.

"Jessie Pearl," she says, "I am so proud of you. But I'm the oldest girl. I should have been there to help."

Just then Vivi starts howling in the bedroom. "That's the reason Frank didn't stop by here," I say. "He knew you were busy with Vivi."

Anna's baby is only ten months old. Anna goes to check on Vivi and comes back carrying her. With blond curls and big blue eyes, she's as pretty as a doll.

Anna pulls a rocking chair close to the stove's warmth and settles Vivi to her breast. "Jessie," she says, "I know how you hate missing school, but you should take a week off to help Carrie. It'll be a while before she gets her strength back."

I do hate missing school, but we have to take care of each other. We promised Ma. "Carrie was coughing again this morning," I say.

Anna's brows knit together. "Carrie's run-down from her pregnancy. We need to be sure she gets enough rest."

When Vivi finishes her breakfast, she reaches her chubby arms toward me. I take her from Anna, bounce her on my lap, and sing:

"Vivi Speas went to town
Riding a billy goat, leading a hound.
The hound dog barked
And the billy goat jumped
And threw Vivi Speas straddle a stump!"

At the end I grip Vivi under her arms, spread my knees, and let her bottom fall through. She laughs.

"I remember singing that song to you," Anna says. "It doesn't seem that long ago and now you're fourteen years old." Anna, Carrie, and Tom were already teenagers when I was born. I've been tagging behind them my whole life.

From a peg by the door, Anna takes her coat and a wool shawl to wrap Vivi in. "Let's go see that new baby!"

Carrie clasps Anna to her chest in a bear hug. "I'm so glad you're here," she says. "My milk hasn't come in yet. I'm afraid Ky's hungry, and..." Her voice drops to a whisper. "I'm so sore, down there."

Anna nods sympathetically. "My milk didn't come in for a couple of days after I had Vivi. That's perfectly natural, and I know just what you mean about down there."

I scoop Vivi up into my arms. "The two of us are going to play in the parlor. Since I'm never having a baby, I don't need to hear all the gory details."

Both my sisters howl with laughter. "Did Jessie tell you she fainted when Ky was born?" Carrie asks.

"No," Anna says. "I believe she left that part out."

"Of course she did," Carrie continues. "But I think it's time our Jessie knew about babies. She and Joe Thompson have been making calf eyes at each other."

Anna stares at me and says in her bossiest voice, "Always be a good girl. A man won't buy a cow if he can get the milk for free."

My face feels hot and I tug on my braid. "Don't be ridiculous," I snap at her. "I got no interest in boys. At least not like that. I'm going to teachers' college."

Carrie raises her eyebrows and smirks. "Jessie, you're protesting way too much. I'd bet my bottom dollar you'll forget all about school the same way Ma did. You'll marry J.T. and have a baby of your own someday."

I hold Vivi in the crook of my arm and slam the door. J.T. is just my hunting and fishing buddy—or at least that's all I'm admitting to.

I'm standing on the back porch staring off into the woods when J.T. finds me. "A penny for your thoughts, Jessie."

"Ah, they're not worth a penny. I was just feeling restless."

He reaches into his coat pocket and pulls out a sack of peppermints. My favorite.

I stand on my tiptoes and give him a quick peck on the cheek. With his straw-colored hair and grass-green eyes, he's even better than candy. "Thank you kindly. I have a big sweet tooth."

He grins. "Since I walked all the way to Frank Meyers's store, don't I deserve a real kiss?"

"That depends. Did you take lemon drops to Liza?"

J.T. shakes his head. "Jessie, you're the only girl I'm buying candy for."

3 | A ONE-ROOM SCHOOL

On his way out, Frank leans over and kisses Carrie's cheek. "Me and your pa won't be home for lunch," he says. "We're gonna help Tom with his plant beds. Toward the end of the week, he'll return the favor."

Carrie reaches up and touches his arm. "Don't be late for supper," she says. She takes a sip of her morning coffee and nods in my direction. "Jessie, I'm feeling strong enough for you to go back to school today."

I clear the table and take the breakfast dishes over to the sink. "I don't think you're ready. It's only been three weeks since Ky was born. Yesterday you stayed in bed almost all day."

Carrie coughs and covers her nose and mouth with a handkerchief. "Stop worrying about me," she says. "This is your last year of school. Ma would want you to graduate from eighth grade like the rest of us."

She's right. Ma placed a lot of value on book learning.

Wearing the new sailor dress Anna made for me, I head east, in the opposite direction from Anna and Cole's house. Trudging up Flint Hill Road, I pass by J.T.'s and then come to the Phillipses' farm.

Liza Phillips falls in beside me. "I declare," she says. "Jessie Hennings is wearing a dress."

I ignore her smart mouth. "Morning, Liza."

She puts her nose in the air. "I've told you that I prefer to be called Elizabeth." She reaches out and touches my navy wool coat. "Is this new? I've seen this very coat in the Sears and Roebuck catalogue."

I can tell she's jealous, so I rub it in. "It sure is."

What I don't say is that it's only new to *me*. Anna made it out of Ma's cloak after she died.

Liza is quiet for a few minutes, and I hope she'll stay that way.

We walk by the Pilcher farm, and Billy and Bobby run out to join us. "Y'all best behave today," their ma calls, "or I'll have a hickory stick waitin' when you get back home."

The twins shove each other and race ahead. The way I have it figured, Mrs. Pilcher might as well get the hickory stick ready.

We walk about a mile to my cousin Viney Brown's house. She's waiting for us at the top of the hill. "How is Carrie?" she asks.

"Still worn out from giving birth. To be honest, I'm worried about leaving her alone."

Liza butts in. "Jessie, is that why you haven't been in school or at church on Sunday mornings?"

I kick a can back at the Pilcher boys. "Yep, Carrie had a baby, and I've been looking after her."

Liza sniffs. "Sounds like laziness to me, on both your parts. When my sister had her baby, she was back at work the next day."

That Liza is such a liar. I jump in front of her and poke my finger into her chest. "When my ma was sick, I promised her I'd try to be a lady. But if you say one more word about my sister, I'm gonna knock you on your butt."

"Take your hands off me," Liza says, "or I'll tell the teacher when we get to school."

I push my finger even harder into her chest. "Go ahead and tell," I say. "Miss Wilson already knows you're stuck up and hateful."

Liza knocks my hand aside and marches off in a huff. Viney shakes her head. "It's a pity about Liza. She's a beautiful girl, but then she opens her mouth and ruins it."

I nod and think about Liza's blond hair and big brown eyes. She's filled out in all the right places, too. "I admit she's beautiful, but I still hate her worse than Brussels sprouts."

We arrive at school with ten minutes to spare before the first bell. The older boys are already chopping wood for the potbelly stove. "Let's go inside," Viney says. "Out of the cold."

We overhear Liza talking to the teacher while we're hanging our coats in the cloakroom. "I had a wonderful weekend," she tells Miss Wilson. "Thank you for asking. Joe Thompson walked me home from church. He stayed for Sunday dinner too."

My face heats up and my hands knot into fists. "That's a load of horse manure," Viney whispers. "J.T. was walking with Liza's brother Earl."

"Sssh." I put my fingers to my lips. "I want to hear the rest of this story."

"How is J.T.?" Miss Wilson asks. "I often wonder about my former students."

"He's practically a member of our family," Liza continues. "Joseph and Earl are applying for jobs at the R. J. Reynolds Tobacco Company. I expect they'll both move to Winston and live in a boardinghouse."

Viney squeezes my hand. "Don't pay her no mind," she says.

I nod and follow Viney to our desk, but J.T. is on my mind. He's been talking about moving to Winston ever since tobacco prices fell to twenty-two cents a pound.

Miss Wilson rings the bell, and the boys hustle to their seats on the right side of the room. Girls sit on the left. After everybody's settled, we stand and repeat the Pledge of Allegiance.

Miss Wilson reaches into her desk and takes out a copy of *Little Women*. "I'll read aloud for a few minutes," she says, "before we start recitations."

I already know this story because I borrowed the book from Miss Wilson last year. When she reads the part about Beth dying, I brush away tears. I can just imagine how Jo feels because I love my sisters something fierce.

Miss Wilson finishes reading and calls the first grade to the recitation bench. Viney taps my shoulder. "The Pilcher boys have peashooters," she whispers. I twitch when one catches me square in the back. Peas fly around the room and kids duck for cover. Liza squeals like she's been mortally wounded.

Miss Wilson turns from the blackboard, catching both boys in the act. She holds out her hand. "Bring those to me," she says. "Enough foolishness. One more infraction and I'll be forced to get out my paddle. Jessie, I believe the Pilcher boys are in need of some extra reading instruction. Could you work with them up front?"

"Yes, ma'am, I'd be happy to."

Viney digs me in the ribs. "Teacher's pet," she teases.

At lunchtime, I wait in the schoolroom for a chance to talk with Miss Wilson. She uses her desk as a table and takes a biscuit out of her dinner bucket. She motions for me to sit down. "Jessie, what's on your mind?"

I pace across the room and tug on my braid. "Ma'am, I can't sit down right now. I shouldn't be here." I tell her how weak Carrie has been. "I have this sick feeling in my stomach. I came back to school too soon."

Miss Wilson stands and pats my shoulder. "Jessie," she says, "I've never known you to stay out of school without a valid reason. It's not possible to learn in such a worried state. Go home. See to your sister."

I put on my coat and grab my dinner pail. A cold wind whips my braid back and forth. I take a shortcut, rushing across plowed fields and streaking through the woods. My side aches, and I stop to catch my breath.

When I finally make it home, there's no smoke curling from the chimney. I burst through the front door. The house is ice cold. "Carrie, Carrie," I yell, and barrel into her room.

She gazes up at me from her bed, where she's lying underneath a patchwork quilt. "I fell asleep," she says. "I'll get up in just a minute."

I put my hand against her forehead. She's burning up. I bolt outside again and draw a bucket of water from the well. I fill a glass and hold it to her lips.

"Enough. Enough, Jessie. I'm gonna float away."

I wet a cloth and bathe Carrie's forehead. "Check on Ky," she whispers.

I go over to the cradle and Ky looks up at me. "Hey there, little man," I say softly. "How are you doing?" I reach in and check his diaper. "You're wet, but I can fix that. Your aunt Anna taught me how when Vivi was born."

I change him with my back to Carrie, afraid she'll see the worry in my eyes. "Just to be on the safe side, I'll take Ky to Anna's house. We don't want him to get sick too."

Carrie starts to cry. "I bet Ky's hungry. I slept through his morning feeding. What kind of mother does that?"

"A sick one," I answer. "But lucky for us, Anna will breastfeed him until you're feeling better."

Carrie wipes her eyes and coughs into a handkerchief. "Jessie, what do you think is wrong with me?"

I fight to keep the panic out of my voice. "I'm sure it's nothing serious. Doc probably needs to give you a tonic."

Carrie's head sinks into the pillow, and she closes her eyes.

4 | TB

I grab a blue shawl that Anna knitted and wrap Ky up like a papoose. "Carrie," I say, "just rest. Don't get out of bed until I come back."

I hold tightly to Ky and start the walk to Anna's house. I'm afraid to run. Afraid I'll trip and hurt him. The cold air swirls around my legs, and I wish for long johns and overalls.

Patches runs, panting to catch up with me. I'm grateful for his company. I push the shawl back to check on Ky. He has solemn eyes, like a little old man. "We're almost there," I tell him. "Anna's been taking care of me my whole life. She'll take good care of you too."

I push through the back door without knocking. "Anna, Anna, I need your help!"

She gets up from the rocking chair, clutching her sewing to her chest. "What's wrong, Jessie? You're scaring me."

I pull the shawl away from Ky's head. "Carrie's too sick to feed him."

Anna's sewing falls to the floor. "Where's Frank?"

I thrust the baby into her arms. "He's helping Tom with his plant beds. Take care of Ky while I find him."

Anna nods. "Of course I will. And Jessie," she whispers, "hurry."

Without Ky, I move a lot faster. My brother, Tom, lives about a half mile from here, near Logan's Creek. My nose runs from the cold. My legs ache. I push myself harder, faster.

From a distance, I can see the menfolk stretching white cloth over the plant beds to protect them from cold weather. "Frank, Frank!" I yell.

Frank shades his eyes from the winter sun and takes off running, meeting me halfway. He grabs my shoulders. "What's wrong? Is it Carrie or the baby?"

I bite my lip to keep from crying. "Carrie's running a fever. She needs Doc Benbow."

Frank lets go of me and runs toward Tom's house to get his Model T. I stumble behind him. "Wait for me," I call. "I'll stay with Carrie while you go for the doctor."

Carrie's breathing sounds harsh and wheezy while she sleeps. I let her rest and start supper. Keeping busy should make the waiting go faster.

Pa lets himself in the back door. "Doc will probably stay to supper." He pours some water from the kettle into a pan and washes up. "I'm gonna check on Carrie," he says.

I grease a skillet for cornbread, then fry fatback meat and peel potatoes. I rummage in the canning closet for a jar of green beans.

About twenty minutes later, the front door slams. "Doc, let me take your coat and hat," Frank says. "She's in the room there to your right."

While Doc examines Carrie, I flip the cornbread onto a dinner plate. It's just right, golden brown. I take the beans and potatoes off the stove and slide everything into the warming oven. I make the coffee...and wait.

Patches paws at the back door. I give him the scraps from breakfast. "Sorry, boy. I forgot all about feeding you."

Finally I hear footsteps heading for the kitchen. I pour coffee while Pa, Frank, and Doc Benbow gather around the table.

Doc takes a mug and stirs in some cream. "I wish I had better news," he says.

I stare out the kitchen window, looking away from the fear in Frank's eyes. It reminds me of how he looked after the war. "I think Carrie has tuberculosis," Doc continues. "Of course I need to examine her sputum under a microscope, but that's just to confirm what I already know, in my gut."

Pa sets his mug down too hard, and coffee sloshes over the rim. "There ain't no cure for it, is there, Doc?"

Doc sips his coffee and takes his time answering. "Some people go away to a sanatorium. There are several good ones in Asheville."

"Go away?" Frank's voice breaks. "Away from Ky and me?"

I grip the kitchen counter and pray for strength. "How would they treat Carrie at a sanatorium?" I ask. "Would they give her special medicine?"

"There is no medicine to cure tuberculosis," Doc says. "At a sanatorium, Carrie would rest, spend a lot of time in the fresh air, and eat nutritious meals."

I hear a noise and turn around. Carrie is standing in the kitchen doorway. "I can do all of that at home," she says.

Frank rises to his feet. "Let's get you back to bed, Carrie."

"No!" she says. "This is my life everybody's talking about. I deserve to make the decisions."

Doc nods and looks Carrie square in the eyes. "There are no guarantees," he says. "Though some people get well staying in a sanatorium, others don't."

Carrie nods. "And those people die, right, Doc? Except they die alone, away from the people they love most." A look of determination settles on her face. "I'm going to stay right here," she says. "Since there are no guarantees, I'm going to spend whatever time I have left being Ky's mother."

Doc taps his fingers against the table. "Sleep on it," he says. "You may change your mind. In the meantime, I'll write out instructions for home care." Doc opens his medical bag and takes out a tablet and pencil. "Carrie, like we discussed, you're contagious. Avoid close contact with your family, and no breastfeeding."

All the fight goes out of Carrie and she hangs her head. "Doc, is there a chance I've made Ky sick too?"

Doc's voice is full of concern. "That happens in about half the cases I see. That's why I said no more breastfeeding."

Carrie raises her fist and pushes it against her mouth, but a ragged sob escapes anyway.

Tears snake down Frank's cheeks. He crosses the room and scoops Carrie up in his arms. "I need some time alone with my wife," he says. Carrie's head is bent to her chest, like a broken doll.

Pa hasn't said much during Doc's visit, and my eyes dart in his direction. He frowns. The deep grooves on either side of his mouth sag.

"Hezekiah," Doc says. "With enough rest, some patients beat TB. I'll do everything I can for her. Don't lose hope."

Pa doesn't have to tell me what Carrie's illness means. I'll have to quit school to take care of her. There's nobody else to do it. I turn and take the food out of the warming oven.

"No, none for me," Doc says. "I've got another call to make."

Pa rises from his chair. "Thanks for stoppin' by. Let me walk you to the door." On his way out, he turns to me. "Jessie, you can put away the food. I've got no appetite."

I nod and clean the kitchen. For once I didn't ruin the meal, but nobody has the heart to eat it.

Our house is all shut up like a coffin. Every bit of light and sound is snuffed out by closed doors. Pa's in his room, Frank and Carrie in theirs. I need to talk to J.T.

With only an hour of daylight left, I take the dirt road toward his house. I stop to button my coat and finger-comb my hair. His ma thinks I'm a heathen, way too much of a tomboy. There's no need to give her any more ammunition.

J.T. answers my knock on the door. The smell of fresh-baked cornbread makes my stomach growl. His mama calls, "Who is it?"

His green eyes light up at the sight of me. "It's Jessie, Ma." He reaches for my hand. "Come on in. Out of the cold."

I shake my head. "Could we take a walk instead?"

J.T. nods. "Wait here while I get a lantern. It'll be dark before long."

On the way back toward the main road, he pulls me behind the woodshed. He sets the lantern down and touches my arm. "What's wrong, Jessie? You're trembling."

I can't stop the tears from spilling down my cheeks. "TB. Carrie has TB."

J.T. hugs me. "God, Jessie. I'm as sorry as can be." Then he leans down and kisses the top of my head. His lips feel feather soft. "I hate seein' you so sad," he says.

I wish I could burrow into his arms and hide from Carrie's sickness. "J.T., you know what this means. Tuberculosis is contagious, and Doc wants to make sure it doesn't spread. We can't go hunting or fishing together for a while. I came to say goodbye."

5 | LEPERS

I shade my eyes from the afternoon sun streaming onto our back porch. Anna will be here soon, bringing Ky for his afternoon visit.

"Carrie," I say. "Wake up, sleepyhead. It's almost time."

Carrie gazes up at me from the wide slats of her reclining cure chair. Doc drew Pa a picture, and he modeled it after the ones used in sanatoriums. "Is the water ready?" she asks.

"Yes, of course it is."

She dips her hands in the basin and scrubs them with lye soap. "I have to be extra careful not to infect Ky," she says.

Carrie has said this every afternoon for nearly three months. Winter has turned into spring, and our days have settled into a monotonous routine.

The door slams, and I meet Anna in the kitchen. She hands Ky to me and reaches into the cloth bag slung over her shoulder. "I brought Carrie some pound cake. Maybe you can get her to eat some of it later. She's losing too much weight."

I nod. "I'll try harder to fatten her up, but she doesn't have much of an appetite. She just wants to sleep."

Anna takes Ky from me again and goes out to the back porch. She sits in the chair farthest from Carrie, holding Ky in her lap.

Carrie stares at her baby as if she's starving and he's her last bite of bread. It's a look so raw that I turn away.

"Can I touch him?" she asks.

Anna gets up and stands beside her chair. Carrie reaches out and rubs Ky's leg. She closes her eyes. "His skin's so soft," she says. "I dream about it." She doesn't dare touch Ky's hands for fear he'll put them in his mouth. "I'd give anything to kiss him."

I scrub my sleeve across my eyes. I want to make Carrie better and give Ky back to her.

Anna moves over to her chair again with Ky, and Carrie attempts a smile. "Is Sophie keeping Vivi today?"

Anna nods. "Marrying Sophie was one of the smartest things Tom's ever done. She shows up every afternoon without me even asking."

Carrie leans her head back against the chair. "Ky's getting so big and handsome, just like his daddy."

Anna bounces him on her lap. "He's eating a little solid food now. Applesauce, mashed-up peas, some creamed potatoes."

Carrie reaches into her pocket for a handkerchief. "What else is he doing, Anna?"

"Well, he loves watching Vivi. They play a game where she holds out her rag doll and he reaches for it. Oh, and he can roll over now. Would you like to see?"

"Of course," Carrie says. "Every milestone is precious."

I spread Ky's blanket on the porch floor, and Anna lays him on top of it. He lifts his leg in the air, shifts his body, and flops over onto his tummy.

"That's the cutest thing I've ever seen," Carrie says. She claps for him as if he had just performed a circus trick.

"He's growing like a weed," Anna says, "and doing all the things Vivi did at four months old."

Anna keeps talking, sharing tiny details, until the afternoon sun puts Carrie to sleep. We leave her napping and tiptoe into the kitchen.

"You look exhausted," Anna says.

I shrug. "More like bone tired. Doc told me to keep Carrie's dishes and towels separate. I burn all her handkerchiefs, record her temperature twice a day, empty her sputum cup. And she's too weak to go to the outhouse. There's a lot to do."

"Then sit for a spell," Anna says. "I'll make some coffee." She hands Ky to me and I breathe in his sweet baby smell.

Anna puts the coffee pot on the stove. "Jessie, this is probably the hardest thing you'll ever have to do. I'm proud of you. Ma would be proud too."

I stare at the floor and keep patting Ky's shoulder. "You wouldn't be so proud of me if you knew how I really feel. My back aches like an old woman's. I'm sick of Carrie's hacking cough. It never lets up, not even when she sleeps. Have you looked at my hands?" I hold one in the air. It's scrubbed raw because I'm afraid of getting TB. "And God help me for being so selfish, but I want to finish school and then go away to teachers' college. The way I talked about with Ma."

Anna sets a cup of coffee in front of me. "I'm sorry for the way things have turned out, but there's no help for it right now. Even if Carrie hadn't taken sick, Pa doesn't have the money for teachers' college."

I wish my ma were here. She would find a way to fix things.

Anna places her hand on my shoulder. "Don't be ashamed of the way you're feeling. Your actions are what count."

I take a deep breath to calm down. Ma always told me things have a way of working themselves out. I cling to that thought like a frayed rope.

Anna looks down at Ky with a tender smile. "He's fallen asleep. Why don't you put him in the cradle? That way you can enjoy a piece of cake with your coffee."

After tucking Ky in, I try to think of something pleasant to talk about. "Pa and Frank are cutting the wheat now. I can't wait for the threshing machine to come through. I look forward to it every year."

Anna takes a bite of cake. "The threshers won't eat here this year, or at my house either. They're all worried about catching TB. Sophie's offered to cook for them at her place."

I picture the big threshing machine spouting a cloud of dust. I think about the men swapping labor, following the machine from farm to farm, and of the housewives, each trying to outdo her neighbors by cooking up a feast bigger than the one before.

"Tuberculosis has made lepers out of us," I say. "Like in the Bible."

"It does feel that way," Anna agrees. "But it could be worse. Ky is growing big and healthy. At least he didn't get sick too."

Carrie coughs, and the sound echoes through the kitchen. "You'd best take Ky and go. I should make a mustard poultice for her cough."

Anna rises and slings the cloth bag over her arm. "Jessie," she says, "Carrie will get better." But her voice catches.

I gather up the cups and turn toward the sink. "No matter how hard I try, she just keeps getting worse."

Tears shine in Anna's eyes. "I understand how you feel," she says. "Remember that I was the one nursing Ma."

I grip the sink and pray for strength. What happened to Ma caused enough sadness to last us a lifetime. I'll do whatever it takes to save Carrie.

6 | OLD SATAN HERSELF

Patches is raising a ruckus, running circles around Maude Patterson. I watch from Carrie's bedroom window as she walks toward our house wearing a gray dress that almost touches the ground.

"It's the granny woman," I tell Carrie. "Old Satan herself. She's lugging a carpetbag. Must be roasting in this July heat."

Carrie coughs and says from behind her handkerchief, "Go see what she wants. And mind your manners."

I trot up the driveway to meet Maude. "It's nice to see you, but we weren't expecting company."

She looks at me as if I'm simpleminded. "Call off your fool dog," she says. "I ain't company. I come to stay."

Puzzled, I scratch my head. "You'd best go back home. Carrie has tuberculosis, and Doc's worried about her germs infecting other people."

Maude puts her hands on her hips and snorts. "I'm nigh a hundred years old, and I ain't never seed a germ yet."

I know better than to explain that germs are tiny and that you can only see them under a microscope. "Maude, we don't have any babies that need birthing."

She shoves her carpetbag into my hands. "Carry this to the house. That fool doctor done took most of my midwifin' business. I'm nursin' consumptives now."

Oh, good Lord! I shield my eyes from the sun and look in every direction, but there's no car to take Maude back home. "How did you get here? You couldn't have walked all the way from Siloam."

She doesn't answer me, just keeps moving toward the house. "I'm goin' in," she says. "After I have a drink of water, maybe I'll answer your questions. You sure are a nosy young'un."

Maude strolls in like the Queen of Sheba and sticks her head in Carrie's room. "Heard you was feelin' poorly. I 'spect you need some expert nursin', and I done a heap of it in my time."

Moving past Maude, I trudge down the hall to my room and drop the carpetbag on the floor. Since Frank's staying in the room we keep for company, she'll have to sleep with me. I'd rather have a big old boil on my butt.

While Maude rustles up supper, Carrie plays "The Ballad of Barbara Allen" on her dulcimer. "It seems those songs are always about broken hearts and dying," I say. "I wish you'd play something happy."

Carrie's voice sounds hoarse, and she lays her dulcimer aside. "I'm glad Maude is here," she says.

I frown at her. "Should I take your temperature again? Crazy talk like that is usually caused by a fever."

Carrie giggles. "No, but you've been so busy taking care of me that we haven't had enough time just to talk and read."

I squeeze Carrie's hand. "I'll read to you more often. I promise."

She closes her eyes for a moment. "I'm so lonely and afraid," she whispers.

I climb in bed beside her and she rests her cheek against my chest. "Don't be scared," I say. "I'm right here, and I'll take good care of you. Remember our promise to Ma."

Carrie's body trembles at the mention of Ma. "Jessie," she says, "what do you think heaven's like?"

I shake my head. "I don't know. But neither of us is going there anytime soon. Let's talk about something happy."

Carrie's eyes remain closed, but tears leak out of the corners. "Please, Jessie. I've been thinking about it a lot. Tell me what you think heaven's like."

I close my eyes to block out Carrie's tears. "Let me try and picture it," I say. My mind drifts, sinking into a comfortable place. "Heaven smells like fresh-baked biscuits. Only you don't have to bake them."

Carrie giggles.

"Hey, no laughing," I say. "And sound. Heaven sounds like the lullaby you sang to Ky on the morning he was born."

"It sounds full of love," Carrie says.

"Exactly. But mostly, you *feel* heaven."

"Jessie, what does it feel like?"

"It feels safe and warm, like being rocked in Ma's arms."

I open my eyes and Carrie is looking up at me.

"Sorry, but I didn't see any mansions or streets of gold in my heaven," I tell her.

Tears glisten on her cheeks. "Don't be sorry, Jessie. Your heaven sounds perfect."

Maude cooks Carrie's favorite meal for supper: chicken pie, mashed potatoes, and green beans. "It smells wonderful," Carrie says as Frank helps her into her chair.

"Now don't overdo it," he says. "The minute you're tired, let me know."

It's a treat for us to have supper with Carrie. She usually says no, afraid she'll be sick at the table.

"Didn't you get my letter tellin' you not to come?" Pa asks Maude. "Doc says tuberculosis is contagious."

"I got your letter," she says. "But I ain't worried about consumption. When the good Lord decides it's my time, he'll take me. And I won't leave this world a day before."

"I don't know how much I can afford to pay you," Pa says. "It all depends on tobacco prices."

Maude wags her chin. "I'm sure we can strike a fair deal."

I take a big bite of chicken pie and it melts in my mouth. Maude is a world-class cook. I'll give her that much.

Pa leans his good ear toward Maude. "Who'd you say dropped you off?"

She wrinkles her nose. "It was that fool son-in-law of mine. He's so afraid of consumption that he let me out at the turnoff to Flint Hill Road. Wouldn't drive one bit closer."

Carrie puts her hand on her chest. "I'm wasting away. No wonder people are afraid."

I look down at my plate, not sure what to say. Carrie's arms and legs are stick-thin now. Her skin is sickly pale and her eyes ringed by dark circles.

"You have to eat more and build your strength back up," Frank says.

Pa takes seconds of the chicken pie and then passes it to Carrie. Maude smiles at them. "Cookin' is one of my talents. Course I have lots of other ones too."

"Like modesty," I say. Frank's lips twitch, and he hides his face in his napkin. Carrie kicks me under the table. Luckily, Pa didn't hear, or he'd give me a talking-to about my manners.

Maude squints her beady eyes at me. "I'm sendin' Jessie to work at the tobacco barn tomorrow," she says. "With Carrie sick and Jessie takin' care of her, you're bound to be shorthanded."

Maude thinks she's punishing me for my smart mouth, but she couldn't be more wrong. Still, I feel guilty and look for Carrie's approval.

She winks at me. "That's good thinking," she says to Maude. "And you should make Jessie spend the day fishing on Saturday. Wouldn't a mess of fried fish taste delicious?"

Maude purses her lips. "I'm on to you girls. Don't think you're pullin' the wool over my eyes." She points at Frank. "Take Carrie back to bed and get her settled." And then her crooked finger points at me. "Missy, I did the cookin', so you can do the washin' up."

7 | TOBACCO SEASON

Carrie is still sleeping when I leave for the tobacco barn. It's barely light out, and the grass is wet with dew. I feel like our mule Patience, when she's turned out to pasture after spending all winter in the barn.

Tom, Pa, and Frank have already started priming the tobacco. Bent nearly double, they move through the field, breaking off the big green leaves at the bottom of the stalk. "Sophie and Anna are waiting for you!" Tom hollers. Spreading my arms wide, I spin around, breathing in the smells of fresh air, sticky tar, and red clay soil.

I hurry toward the tobacco barn with Patches running ahead of me. "Good morning, Jessie," Sophie calls. She and Anna stand close together underneath the barn's open-air shelter. Nearby, Vivi and Ky play on a pallet made of patchwork quilts.

"Good morning, ma'am," I say to Sophie. She was my teacher before she married Tom, and I can't get used to calling her by her first name.

"Sophie has some good news," Anna tells me.

This can only mean one thing. I smile and point at her tummy. Sophie laughs and her light-freckled skin turns pink. "Tom and I are expecting," she says. I hug her tight because I know how much this baby means to them.

"That's the best news I've heard in a month of Sundays," I say. "Tom must be proud as a peacock."

Sophie nods. "He is. It would be perfect if only Carrie felt better."

Just the mention of her name makes me feel guilty. I wish I could share some of my health with her. It's like I have two cookies and Carrie has none.

Anna kneels by the pallet and reaches out her hands to Ky. He pulls himself up. "Good boy," Anna says. "Look, Jessie, he can sit up now."

"Mamamamama!" Ky says.

I gasp. "What? What did he say?"

Sophie smiles. "Calm down, Jessie. He wasn't calling her Mama. Babies just babble. Mamamama, Dadadada. It doesn't mean anything."

I cross my arms and nod. "It's a shock, that's all. I'm afraid hearing him say that will hurt Carrie. She aches for him, says her arms feel empty."

We hear the tobacco sled scraping against the rocky path. Tom lightly slaps the reins against Patience's rump, as she pulls our first sledful of tobacco to the barn. "Jessie, good to see you workin'," he says as he bends over to unhitch Patience from the sled.

"Congratulations on the new baby! You're my favorite brother."

Tom ducks his head. He's shy, but he has a kind way about him, like Pa. "Is that because I'm your only brother?" he asks.

"Exactly right," I say.

He winks at me, then turns toward Sophie. "Don't overdo it today. You hear?"

"I'll take extra care," Sophie promises.

Tom gives his wife a tender smile before heading back to the field with Patience. "Giddyup, you ornery mule!"

I put a tobacco stick between the two notches on the tie horse. "Take your pick," Anna says. "Would you rather tie or hand up?"

"Tie," I say.

Anna and Sophie take the tobacco from the sled in bunches. They hand it to me three or four leaves at a time, and I tie it to the stick with twine. There's a real art to tying. I have to loop the tobacco tight so it will hold to the stick, but not so tight that it cuts the leaves.

"How is Carrie this morning?" Anna asks.

I loop the twine around the tobacco, and it coats my hands with a sticky brown gum. "She was still sleeping when I left."

I tie tobacco across the stick, leaving just enough space on each end for my hands. Spreading my arms wide, I take the heavy stick off the tie horse and start a pile. When the men finish in the field, they'll hang the sticks in the barn and fire up the furnace. Heat cures the tobacco, dries it out, so that it turns a golden color.

Anna drops a handful of leaves and races over to the pallet. "Vivi Speas, spit that out of your mouth! No eating dirt!" Anna makes her spit, then pulls a handkerchief from her pocket and wipes Vivi's mouth.

Sophie chuckles. "Those two are a handful. How about you, Jessie? How are you holding up?"

I make sure Anna is busy before answering. "I'm sad I had to quit school, and I'm scared. I bet Carrie doesn't weigh even a hundred pounds. She's so hoarse now that she can't sing."

Sophie nods. "I'm sorry about school, Jessie. I know how much it means to you. I've been selfish and stayed away from Carrie because of my pregnancy." She hands me a bunch of tobacco and then pats her stomach. "After what happened to Violet, this baby means the world to Tom and me." Violet died five years ago from diphtheria, and until now, Sophie hasn't been able to get pregnant again.

"I understand, and Carrie will too." What I don't say is that I'm worried about myself. Being in such close contact with Carrie is dangerous.

From the end of July until mid-September, we work like pack mules. The men prime four days a week, and I help Anna and Sophie at the tobacco barn. The other two days we sucker the tobacco, breaking off the new sprouts that would suck the strength from the plant. By the end of the season, my palms are stained the color of snuff.

Sundays are my only free day. I usually read to Carrie on the back porch while Maude and the menfolk nap.

On this September Sunday, I can tell she isn't paying attention. "Jessie," she says, interrupting me, "let's read about Jane and Mr. Rochester another day. Would you go to my room and get a tablet and pencil from my top bureau drawer?"

"Why? Are we writing a book?" I ask, jokingly.

Carrie shifts in her reclining chair and looks away from me. "No, Jessie. I want you to write down everything I'm about to tell you. After I die, you can read it to the family."

Shocked, I let the book tumble to the floor. "No! I—I can't. Promise me you'll try harder to get well. Promise me!"

"I can't try any harder," Carrie says. "I don't even have the strength left to play my dulcimer or write a letter. How long do you think I can go on? I've prayed, but sometimes the answer to a prayer is no."

I sink to my knees beside her chair. "What about me?" I ask. "It'll break my heart if you die. Promise me you won't give up."

Carrie reaches out and touches my hair. "Don't cry, Jessie. I don't know what I was thinking. There's no need to write a letter. I'm just feeling blue."

8 | J.T.

Maude's snoring sounds like a whistling teakettle. Burying my head in the pillow, I try to drown it out. But instead of silence, I hear Carrie's voice. *How much longer do you think I can go on?*

When I can't stand it another minute, I slip out of bed and pull on a cotton shirt and overalls. After sneaking out the back door, I light the lantern and whistle for Patches. "Come on, boy! I need to see J.T."

The farmyard is black as pitch, and my shadow looms in the lantern light. I haven't left our land in seven months, not since my last day of school. A couple of times Pa mentioned that J.T. asked about me at Frank Meyers's store. But Pa told him what he tells everybody. "Best stay away. Doc says it's contagious, and we don't want it spreadin' through the community."

The road to J.T.'s stretches in front of me as dark as a root cellar. It's deserted except for the occasional possum and the outline of overhanging pine trees. A tingling starts along my scalp and creeps down my spine. "There's nothing to be afraid of," I whisper. An owl screeches from the deep woods. I think about the headless horseman and Ichabod Crane.

When I finally see the Phillipses' farm up ahead, I breathe a huge sigh of relief. I clutch my chest until my heartbeat returns to normal. Veering off the main road, I take the path to J.T.'s house. His room is on ground level, to the right of the front porch. I walk around and peer in the open window. His bed is pushed up against it.

"J.T.," I whisper. "J.T., it's me."

When he doesn't answer, I grab a stick lying in the front yard. Reaching in, I prod him in the back. "J.T.! It's me."

"Jessie?" He scrambles to his knees and looks out. "Girl, are you crazy?" he says in a low voice. "Put that stick down, and I'll be right out."

Soon J.T. is climbing over the windowsill. He takes the lantern from my hand, turns down the wick, and sets it on the front porch. In the moonlight, he reaches out and strokes my cheek. "I've missed you, Jessie."

My heart strums a lonesome ballad. "I've missed you too."

J.T. bends down and lightly kisses my lips. Then he straightens up and says, "When I kiss you, you're supposed to close your eyes."

"But...but you've never kissed me on the lips before. Nobody's ever kissed me there." I look up at J.T. and wonder if the yearning inside of me shows on my face. "Why'd you wait until tonight to do that?"

J.T. laughs and kisses the end of my nose. "Sweet pea, I'm three years older than you. I've been waitin' on you to grow up." He touches my shoulder. "Jessie, what are you doing here in the middle of the night, anyway?"

I tug on my braid and stare at the ground. Usually being around J.T. is as comfortable as my favorite pair of overalls, but that kiss has left me dumb as a post. I tell him the simple truth. "Because I'm afraid Carrie's dying, and that my heart will split wide open if she does."

J.T. scuffs his bare toes in the grass. "The only reason I've stayed away," he says, "is because your pa told me to. I waited for you every Sunday afternoon by the fishing hole, but you never came."

"I read to Carrie on Sunday afternoons, while everyone else naps."

"I can see why," J.T. says. "You're afraid time with her is runnin' out." He bends to relight the lantern. "Come on. I'd best walk you home before your pa gets a shotgun after me."

As we make our way, J.T. carries the lantern with his right hand and holds mine with his left. "It was spooky walking to your house," I tell him. "So quiet and dark."

"And how does it feel now?" he asks.

"Like we're on an adventure. It's not scary when you're with me."

J.T. squeezes my hand. "You shouldn't be out late by yourself. I'm pretty sure Liza's uncle Wade has a still. Talk is, Rafe Allman is runnin' shine for him."

We creep through the farmyard to my back porch. Light shines from the kitchen window. "We've been caught red-handed," I whisper.

J.T. nods. "I'd best come in with you. It looks like we've got some explainin' to do."

When I push the back door open, Pa sets his coffee cup down on the table. Maude peers at me through her spectacles. I don't waste a minute worrying about her, but one look at Pa tells me I'm in deep trouble.

J.T. steps in front of me. "Sir," he says, "could you and I talk about this outside?"

Pa shakes his head. "Nope. I want to hear what my daughter has to say for herself. You and Jessie have a seat and tell me what's goin' on here."

I take a deep breath. "Pa, Carrie asked me to write a letter to be read after she dies. I didn't want to worry anybody else in the family. All I could think of was telling J.T. because he's my best friend."

Pa stares at J.T., and it's a look mean enough to stop a panther in his tracks. "Did anything happen tonight between you and my daughter?"

J.T. stares right back at Pa. He copies me and speaks loudly so Pa can hear. "No sir. I wouldn't do anything to hurt Jessie. I plan to marry her someday."

Marry?

Pa glares at J.T. "And when would 'someday' be?"

I've never heard my pa sound so stern. Maybe he can tell I've been kissed.

J.T. glares right back at Pa. "When Jessie's eighteen," he says. "That'll give me time to save some money so I can take care of her."

The two of them talk about me like I'm a horse about to be traded. I hold up my hands. "Wait a dad-burned minute! I'm planning to be a teacher before I settle down. Who said anything about marriage?"

J.T. gives me a slow, lazy smile. "Jessie, I didn't exactly plan tonight. You reached in my window and prodded me out of bed with a stick. Then we went traipsing around in the dark. Your pa wants to know my intentions."

"Jessie needs a whuppin' for sneaking out!" Maude says. "It's time somebody took her in hand."

Pa's lips twitch like he thinks something's funny. "Maude is right. It's time somebody took Jessie in hand. J.T., are you applyin' for the job?"

"Yes sir, I am."

"All right then. If you're willin' to wait three years, I'll give you my blessin'."

"Dad-burn it! I didn't say yes!"

Pa ignores me and takes a long swig of his coffee. "J.T.," he says, "I'm about to ask you a favor, man to man. Doc says Carrie's contagious, and so I'm askin' you to stay away from here for a while."

"You have my word on it," he says.

Then Pa turns to me. "Jessie, you can't go lookin' for him either."

"Yes sir. You have my word too...until Carrie's better."

Pa stands and helps Maude to her feet. "Let's give Jessie a few minutes alone with her beau."

Maude scowls and crosses her arms. "Hmph, some people are too blind to see what's right in front of them."

J.T. raises his eyebrows.

I shrug. I figure most people see what they want to see. Maude thinks I need a switching, and Pa thinks I need a husband. Neither one of them is right, but I do want J.T. to kiss me again. Soon.

9 | SEASON'S END

Patience stands hitched to the wagon along with Tom's mule, Pudge. Making trips back and forth to the pack house, I help load the tobacco for October market. It's a golden color now, after being cured at high temperatures and separated by grade.

"I'll miss the trip to Winston," Frank says, "but I'd best stay close to home." What he doesn't say is that Carrie is weaker. He just puts on a brave face and ignores it, like the rest of us.

"I bet you won't miss sleepin' in the wagon," Tom says. It'll take Pa and Tom all day to reach Pace's Warehouse. If they can pull in around 4:00 this afternoon, they'll get a ticket to sell the tobacco tomorrow morning.

"No, I won't miss the sleepin' arrangements," Frank says. "But I will miss hearin' the auctioneer and the banjo pickin' outside."

Pa works in silence until the wagon is fully loaded. "That's all she'll hold," he says. "Frank, take care of Carrie. I wish we didn't have to go."

Frank nods. "I'll do everything I can for her."

Pa climbs into the wagon and takes the reins. "C'mon, Tom, it's time to get on the road."

In the lantern light, I stand beside Frank until the wagon fades from sight. He lets out a weary sigh. "We need to do up the mornin' chores," he says. His easy smile is gone, and he doesn't tease me much anymore. A couple of times, I've even smelled moonshine on his breath. "Would you rather do the feedin' or the milkin'?"

Slopping the smelly hogs is my least favorite job. "I'd rather milk," I say, but the dark circles under Frank's eyes tug at my heart. "On second thought, I can handle all the morning chores. Go spend some time with Ky."

"Are you sure? It'll take you twice as long."

"Yes, I'm sure. I got nothing better to do."

He nods and gives me a sad smile. "You're a good sister-in-law, Jessie Pearl."

The chores take me most of the morning. On my way inside, I notice the leaves are turning shades of gold and rust. Hard to believe it's October already. I close the back door and tiptoe through the house in case Carrie is sleeping. Pausing outside her room, I hear somber voices.

"I didn't mind writin' the letter," Maude says. "I've done seen it all. My husband's dead, and two of my children. I'd go in your place if I could."

I lean my back against the wall and slide down beside the door. Carrie coughs so hard that it's painful just to listen to. "I appreciate it, Maude. I really do. Can you read it back to me?"

"*Dear Family,*" Maude begins. "*I've spent a lot of time lying on the porch, and our backyard is full of beauty. In the spring, the sun shone so bright and warm that I could almost see the grass turn green. In the summer, I listened to the threshing machine and the men calling to each other. I sipped lemonade, all sweet and sour at the same time. And now it's my last fall season. I've watched the maple trees, and their crimson leaves are so colorful that I stare at them for hours. Before I was sick, I didn't take enough time to enjoy the wonder that was all around me.*

"*The third chapter of Ecclesiastes has meant a lot to me during the last few months. 'For everything there is a season, and a time for every purpose under heaven.' I'm not sure why I had so few seasons, but I do know that I've been blessed.*

"*Frank, my last thought on this earth will be of you. I prayed so hard for you to come back to me after the Great War, and then all I wanted was to give you a son. God answered those prayers. The morning Ky was born was the happiest day of my life. Cherish your memories of me, but someday it will be time to lock those memories away and give your heart to someone else. Choose your second wife wisely. Be sure she can love our son with all her heart.*

"*Ky, that I won't live to see you grow up is my biggest regret. Someday you will probably be curious about me. Of course your father can answer most of your questions, but also talk with my sisters. Sometimes men have a way of not noticing all the details, and Anna and Jessie can help fill in what's missing.*

"*There are many things I wanted to teach you—how to rest your head against a cow's belly when you milk her, how to thump a watermelon to tell when it's ripe, how playing the dulcimer can help you forget your troubles. Before I got sick, people always said I had a beautiful singing voice. There's no way you'll remember, but I sang lots of lullabies to you.*"

Carrie is sobbing now, and I'm sorry as can be for eavesdropping. I reach into my pocket for a handkerchief as Maude struggles toward the end.

"Dearest Pa, you have a kind way about you and have always worked so hard to provide for our family. I sometimes took it for granted and didn't say thank you as often as I should have. It's been hard watching you grieve since Ma died. Please help Frank for me when he faces the same kind of sadness.

"Brother Tom, thank you for always being my protector. Remember killing the copperhead snake when we were kids? And the time you punched David Doub for putting my braid in the inkwell? Anna always says, 'The best thing Tom ever did was marry Sophie.' I don't know if it's the best thing you ever did, but it's close. Both of you deserve so much happiness. I don't know what heaven's like, but I believe I'll see your little Violet there and Ma too."

Maude pauses and draws a deep breath. Her voice sounds shaky when she starts reading again.

"Anna, sister and friend, my earliest memories are of the two of us together. I remember when we learned to swim in the creek, the time Ma whipped us for having a flour fight, and the way we treated Jessie like a doll when she was little. I want to thank you again for taking care of Ky. There's no way I can ever repay you, but you know that I would have done the same for you.

"And finally, to my baby sister, Jessie—"

I bite my fist to keep from making any noise. On tiptoes I creep down the hall and out the back door. I run toward the creek, with Patches beside me. Though we race until my sides ache, I can't outrun what's coming. If there's a God in heaven, I don't understand why he doesn't help us.

10 | LOOK HOMEWARD, ANGEL

Corn is piled up higher than my head in front of the feed barn. Before Carrie took sick, neighbors would help us with the corn shucking every November, and we'd travel throughout the community helping all of them in return.

"It'll just take a few days," Pa says. "Instead of shuckin' the neighbors' corn, we'll stay close to home and work on our own."

Frank smells of moonshine and rips into each husk like a prize-fighter. "It don't matter," he says. "Nosy neighbors would just get on my nerves."

I reach for another ear of corn and hold my tongue. I'll miss the potluck suppers and the fiddle music. A corn shucking always turns into a celebration.

Tom reaches into his back pocket for a bandana and wipes the sweat from his face. "Frank," he says, "if you want to knock off and spend time with Carrie, the rest of us can pick up the slack."

Frank jerks his arm back and throws an ear of corn at Tom. It bounces off his shoulder. "Are you sayin' I'm slack?"

Tom raises his head and looks Frank in the eyes. "No, that's not what I'm sayin'. And you know better too. That's just the liquor talking."

Pa rises up to his full height and moves in front of Frank. "Son, I've ignored the liquor because I understand what you're goin' through. But it's time you and me had a private talk in the barn."

Frank follows Pa, with his head drooping like a hound dog. When they are out of earshot, I say to Tom, "This family is falling apart."

Tom keeps shucking corn like a slow, methodical machine. "Jessie, grief does ugly things to a person. Let Pa handle it."

When we go to wash up, Doc is sitting at the kitchen table. "I've invited him to stay for supper," Maude says.

Pa pours water from the kettle into a basin so we can all wash up. "Good," he says. "I always enjoy Doc's company."

Maude spoons cabbage and pinto beans onto our plates and serves the men first. "I stopped by earlier to check on Sophie," Doc says. "She's round as a butterball. I'm predicting a Christmas baby." "That would be a real blessing," Pa says.

I crumble crackling cornbread into my beans. Though Doc's trying hard not to ruin the meal, we're all afraid.

"Eat up," Maude says. "Surely somebody would like seconds." Pa and I both shake our heads. "No, none for me," Frank says.

Doc pats his rounded stomach. "I had a piece of pie with Sophie. I can't eat another bite."

Maude nods in my direction. "Jessie, help me clear the table." While she pours the coffee, I rake the leftovers into a bowl for Patches and stack the plates in the sink.

"Maude, it would be best if you and Jessie leave the dishes for later," Doc says. He clears his throat and looks down at his folded hands. "In my opinion, Carrie only has a few days left. I've given her laudanum to help her rest."

Frank sucks in his breath like he's been punched in the stomach. "Are you sure?"

Doc shakes his head. "There's no way to know for certain. I've seen patients hold on longer than I expected, but I do know the end is near."

Frank scrambles to his feet, knocking over his chair. It crashes to the floor. "Excuse me," he mumbles. The back door slams behind him. He retches so hard I hear him throw up his supper.

I grip the table and my knuckles turn white. "How will it happen?" I ask.

Doc takes a sip of his coffee before answering. "Many tuberculars die in their sleep. If we're lucky, that's what will happen with Carrie."

Tears shine on Pa's cheeks. "What if we're not lucky?"

"She'll hemorrhage. Lose too much blood."

"Have mercy!" says Maude. "God have mercy."

Pa rests his elbows on the table. He rubs his forehead like he did when Ma died. I wish I could help him, but there's no way to fix it. I slip away to Carrie's room and stand in the doorway, watching her sleep. I want to memorize everything about her—the sound of her voice, the way she smells, how soft her hair feels. Maybe if I stare long enough, my memories of Carrie won't fade like an old quilt. I want them to stay with me always, like my memories of Ma.

While I'm washing up the supper dishes, Frank tugs on my braid. "Jessie, I've moved my clothes back into Carrie's room."

I give the frying pan a final scrub. "Frank, that's a boneheaded move. Doc says she's contagious."

"I need to spend these final days with my wife," he says. "I can't promise her she won't die"—his voice catches—"but I can promise her she won't die alone."

Frank treats Carrie as tenderly as if she were a newborn baby. He bathes her face and spoons soup into her mouth. I hope someday I'll have a husband who loves me half as much.

I rap my knuckles on the door. "Can I come in? I've brought a fresh stack of handkerchiefs and some sage tea. Thought it might help her hoarseness."

Frank motions me in, and both he and Carrie seem at peace. "We've been talkin' about the day we met."

I move over to place the tea on Carrie's bedside table. Her Bible lies open, with Matthew 6:27 circled. *And which of you by being anxious can add one cubit unto the measure of his life?*

Carrie notices me reading the verse. "I don't want to waste a minute I have left being unhappy," she says. "Worrying won't change anything. I think that's what the Bible's saying."

I collect Carrie's used handkerchiefs so that I can burn them. "I'm glad," I whisper. "Glad your faith is helping you." I want to ask how she can be at peace when it feels like somebody is ripping out my heart. But that would only make things worse. I leave the two of them alone.

Maude sits at the kitchen table, picking out the broken beans from a pile of dried pintos. She looks up and studies my face. "You need some fresh air," she says. "Good thing it's washday."

Frank only leaves Carrie's room to go to the outhouse. Except for Sophie, each member of our family visits with Carrie every day. Nobody wants to leave unfinished business.

On the fifth day Anna pulls a chair up to the kitchen table and sits with Maude and me. "I'm exhausted," she says. "I think it's the strain of what's happening to Carrie. Most afternoons a wave of tiredness washes over me, and it's all I can do to hold my head up."

Maude reaches for a cup and pours Anna some coffee. "My coffee is good and strong. It should put a spring in your step."

Anna takes a sip and then turns toward me. "Jessie, you've been so quiet and withdrawn."

I shrug. "What's there to say?"

The next morning I rub sleep from my eyes and make a pot of sage tea. "After you take that to Carrie, I could use some help with breakfast," Maude says.

"Okay, I'll only be a minute."

Outside the bedroom door, I hear Frank crying.

"Can I come in?" I ask.

He doesn't answer. I know in my heart what's on the other side of the door. I turn the knob. He's cradling Carrie in his arms.

I set the tea on her bedside table. Carrie's eyes are closed, her body stiff and still. Dried blood stains her mouth and the front of her shift.

Frank clutches Carrie closer. "She died alone," he sobs. "I fell asleep."

My knees give out and I sink to the floor. A blizzard inside of me sends ice water rushing through my veins. My teeth chatter. "Oh, dear God."

11 | BARE BONES

"Jessie. Jessie girl." Maude's voice comes to me through a fog. Then she slaps my face. Once. Twice. Three times.

I grab hold of her wrist. "Stop it. Just go away."

Maude sighs. "I wish I could, Jessie, but we have to get Carrie's body ready for burial."

I close my eyes and remember when Ma died. By the time I saw her, Carrie and Anna had her laid out in her Sunday best. Maude hands me a wet cloth to wipe my face. "Tell me what to do," I whisper.

"Just watch," Maude says. "That way you'll know what to do next time."

"Next time? What do you mean by that?"

"With the grim reaper, there's always a next time," Maude says. She rises and cuts the bloody shift off Carrie's body.

I shudder at how TB picked the flesh from her bones.

"Go over to the closet," Maude says, "and get Carrie's wedding dress. She chose it for her buryin' outfit."

I hold the dress up, remembering how happy Carrie was on her wedding day. I touch the soft cotton voile and the Cluny lace on the skirt. "She was a beautiful bride," I say.

Maude starts with Carrie's face and bathes her in warm water. She puts clean underclothes on her. "Help me, Jessie, so I won't tear her dress." I help Maude put Carrie's stiff arms through the sleeves. "Don't be so skittish," Maude says. "It's all right if you touch her."

My hands shake as I comb and fluff her hair. "She's lost more than thirty pounds. It's a miracle that the dress fits."

"Ain't no miracle involved," Maude says. "When all of you was workin' in tobacco, Carrie had me take up her dress."

I drop the comb and it clangs against the floor. "It took guts to plan her own service and say her goodbyes. I don't know how she did it."

Maude touches my cheek. "Your color don't look good," she says, "and your legs are wobblin'." She wraps her strong arms around me. "Let yourself grieve, Jessie. Losin' a sister is a terrible thing."

Maude holds on tight, but there are no tears inside of me. Just weariness, and a feeling that this is all a bad dream.

Maude pats my back. "The good Lord lets grief in little by little," she says. "He'll help you, Jessie Pearl. If you'll let him."

Finally she holds me at arm's length and peers into my eyes. "I think some fresh air would do you good," she says. "Run tell Anna what's happened. While you're gone, Frank can have some time alone with Carrie."

I grab an old coat that Tom outgrew and let myself out the back door. The wind makes a moaning sound like it's grieving too. I whistle for Patches and race down the dirt road. Carrie will never move again, and knowing that pushes me to run for both of us.

As I open Anna's back door, she and Cole are just sitting down to breakfast. "Hey, Jessie," Cole says. "Grab a plate. Anna's made plenty."

Lifting my head, I look into my sister's eyes. Her hand flies to her mouth. "She's gone. Isn't she, Jessie? Carrie's gone."

I can't say the words, but Anna knows. She stands and we cling to each other like tangled vines. Cole insists that I have some coffee and sausage gravy. I shake my head no.

"I've got Carrie's coffin ready," he says. "Your pa asked me to make it last week."

I break away from Anna and storm at Cole. "Stop it! You hear me? Just stop it! I don't want to hear about Carrie's coffin."

Anna gasps. "Jessie, mind your manners. Cole means well."

I sink into one of the kitchen chairs and bury my face on the table.

Cole finishes the rest of his breakfast in silence. His feelings are hurt, but I'm sobbing too hard to apologize. Anna keeps stroking my hair.

She says to Cole, "It would be a big help if you would go and tell Tom about Carrie. Then stop by Frank Meyers's store. That way the news will spread to all the neighbors."

"I'll do that," Cole says. He puts his hand on my shoulder. "I'm sorry. I didn't mean to make things worse."

———

Maude breathes in through her nose and strips the sheets from Carrie's bed. "Jessie, wind some water from the well," she says, "so I can scrub the sickness out of this room. Death has a powerful odor."

I smell it too. On my way out, Maude hands me the sheets. "I asked Frank to get a fire goin' so we can burn all her linens."

I clutch the sheets to my chest. "Maude, how do we get past something this awful?"

She shakes her head. "Ain't no secret to it, Jessie. You just have to keep on living."

"I can't hardly stand to burn her things," Frank says. "It's like we're tryin' to wipe out that she was ever here."

I throw the armload of linens in the fire before either of us has time to change our mind. "Worn-out sheets and towels don't matter," I tell him. "Carrie's in here." I point to my heart.

Frank's jaw clenches. "Don't say another word, Jessie. Because it don't help none. What good does it do to have Carrie in our hearts? It'll just make us miserable. But you know what's killing me the most? Ky won't even remember his mother."

I don't have an answer for that and leave him staring into the fire.

Maude has dinner ready around noon. Except for the sad faces, it could be a holiday with the whole family crowded around the table. I crumble a biscuit in my chicken soup and take a small bite. Bland food is about all we can manage.

"I want a cookie," Vivi says.

Grateful she broke the awful silence, I push away from the table and reach into the cookie jar. "Anybody else want one?"

"Put some on a plate," Maude says, "and pour the coffee. I have a letter from Carrie to read out loud. She had me write it not long before she died. It was her way of sayin' goodbye."

After I take my seat again, Maude starts reading. I listen to Carrie's messages to Frank, Ky, Pa, and Tom. When Maude gets to Anna, I know my turn is coming. Gripping the edge of the table, I brace for Carrie's last words to me.

"And finally, to my baby sister, Jessie. From the moment you were born, Anna and I enjoyed spoiling you. We'd do your chores so that you could run and play. But Jessie, when

I got sick, I found out that you're not a little girl anymore but a strong young woman. I have one final request for you. Soon, it will be time for Ky to come home and live with his father. I'm asking you to be his mother, Jessie, at least until Frank remarries. I want you and Anna to always stay close to my boy. Please look after him because I can't.

"*All my love, Carrie.*"

My fingernails dig into the table like claws. "Pa, can I be excused? I need some time to myself."

A parade of neighbor women approach the house, carrying pie plates and covered dishes. "We thought Maude could use our help cooking for the funeral meal," Pansy Pilcher says.

"Come on in," I say. "Maude's in the kitchen."

We've lived like a colony of lepers for months. I don't know what to say to these women. Their small talk gives me a headache.

I leave them and go into the parlor where Carrie is. I touch the wide boards Pa laid her body on. I lift the camphor-moistened cloth that covers her face. Maude says camphor acts as a preservative, but I don't see why that matters anymore.

Anna walks up from behind and gives me a hug. "Put the cloth back, Jessie. This is not the way you want to remember Carrie. When you think of her, remember how pretty she looked on her wedding day."

I take one last look. "I don't know what to do with myself."

Anna nods. "I could use some help bringing in the kitchen chairs and the ones from the bedrooms. Several of the neighbor women are going to sit up tonight with her body."

I help Anna lug chairs and arrange them in a half circle. "It doesn't seem real," I say. "I've seen Carrie every day of my life, but after tomorrow I'll never see her again. *Poof*—she'll be gone. I can't even conceive of it."

Anna takes a seat and pats the chair beside her. "We'll see Carrie in heaven."

"I wish there was a guarantee of that. Do you really believe it?"

"I think everybody lives with doubt, Jessie, but I'm trying hard to believe. Faith brings me comfort."

It means a lot to Pa that our neighbors put aside their chores and came to pay their respects. The church is overflowing.

"Let us pray," Preacher White says. I close my eyes but don't hear a word of his prayer. My brain has turned into a bees' nest, full of humming.

Bett and Abe Bowman walk to the front of the church with their fiddles. The music does what words couldn't. "Amazing Grace" clears my head and fills my heart. There's not a more mournful song on earth.

"That was beautiful," Preacher White says. "Just beautiful." He pauses for a minute, and when he looks up, his brows are furrowed. "I don't understand," he admits. "Carrie's husband, Frank, asked me why this had to happen. And I told him that it's beyond my understanding."

Preacher White nods to all of us sitting in the family pew. "Keep praying. I know for sure that God hears your prayers and will bring comfort. Now I'd like to read from I Corinthians 13:

"For we know in part, and we prophesy in part; but when that which is perfect is come, that which is in part shall be done away...For now we see in a mirror, darkly; but then face to face; now I know in part; but then shall I know fully even as also I was fully known. But now abideth faith, hope, love, these three; and the greatest of these is love."

Preacher White pauses and wipes his eyes. "These verses tell us there are no easy answers for Carrie's death. Only when we meet our Lord will all our questions be answered."

12 | COMFORT

Our footsteps sound like crunching glass as we tramp across the frozen ground toward the cemetery. My breath comes out in puffs.

When we're all gathered around the gravesite, Preacher White says, "Let's bow our heads for a word of prayer." Some of the men move forward to lower Carrie's coffin into the dark hole. *Ashes to ashes and dust to dust.* I shake my head to clear the dizziness, but the preacher's voice sounds like it's coming from miles away.

My body sways, bumping into Anna. She gives me a startled look, and then somebody catches me from behind. Strong arms circle my waist and crush me against a solid chest. "J.T.," I whisper.

His lips move against my ear. "I've got you, Jessie."

I lean on J.T. and close my eyes.

Bett and Abe Bowman sing "In the Sweet Bye and Bye." The song trickles through the crowd and gains strength.

When the service is over, voices murmur, "I'm sorry for your loss." Hands reach out and pat my shoulders.

J.T. elbows his way through the crowd. "Excuse us. Jessie is feeling poorly." Stopping by the hitching rail, he scoops me up and places me on his pa's wagon seat. I bend over with my head between my knees. J.T. scrambles up beside me and strokes my arm. "Jessie, are you all right?"

"My coat's too hot," I mutter. "I'm suffocating."

J.T. reaches over and fumbles with the buttons. He drags my right arm out of its sleeve and then slides the coat off. When the cold air hits me, some of the dizziness passes.

"Did you have breakfast?" he asks.

"Cinnamon toast, but I threw it up."

"Poor Jessie," he says. "I'll get you home as quick as I can."

J.T. pulls the wagon around, and his parents climb on board. "Jessie's feelin' faint," he says. "She probably needs something to eat."

His mama settles herself in the wagon and pulls a quilt over her legs. "Grief often upsets the stomach," she says. "I remember feelin' sickly when my Aunt Myrtle died."

J.T.'s pa shushes her. "I don't think Jessie needs to hear any more sad talk."

J.T. drives slowly, but his mama complains anyway. "Looks like somebody would fix these roads. Bumps aggravate my rheumatism." I'm tempted to push her right out of the wagon.

By the time J.T. pulls into our farmyard, it's full of horse-drawn vehicles and cars. Mr. Thompson jumps out of the wagon and helps me to the ground. He reaches for Mrs. Thompson next. She hustles me toward the kitchen.

"It'll take the men a while to look after the horses. Have a seat, and I'll make you some peppermint tea," she says.

I sip my drink as Maude bosses the neighbor women around the kitchen. "Pansy, put all the desserts on the porch. We'll bring those in after the meal." Pansy ties an apron over her pregnant stomach and starts moving the desserts.

Next Maude inspects a pan of flaky biscuits. "Priscilla," she says, "these look mouth-waterin'."

"Oh, I didn't make them," Mrs. Phillips says. "My daughter Liza did. She's turnin' out to be a talented cook."

Liza saunters in and hugs her mama. "That's because I had such a wonderful teacher."

Mrs. Phillips smiles and pats Liza's smooth blond hair. "A girl who can cook like my daughter is bound to catch a good husband. And she's smart too. Graduated first in her class."

I choke on a mouthful of tea and Maude slaps me on the back. I had the best grades. Liza is only first because I didn't get to finish.

Maude looks me over. It feels like she can see clear inside of me. "Jessie," she says, "there's a lot of hot air in this kitchen. Cool off outside and call the menfolk to dinner."

Hurrying toward the barn, I see Pa leaning against the fence. I tap him on the shoulder. "Food's ready."

He turns and kisses the top of my head. "Make sure there's plenty of water for everybody to wash up."

The men tramp behind Pa to the kitchen and form a line in front of the basin.

My cousin Viney moseys up beside me and whispers in my ear, "Would you look at that?"

I spin around and see J.T. waiting to wash up, with Liza pressed up close behind him.

"Now, Joseph," she says, "be sure and try my ham biscuits. I know they're one of your favorites."

"Could she get any closer to him?" Viney whispers. "She's like a leech."

I scowl at Viney. "She's worse than a leech, but I can't be bothered with Liza right now. Pa would never forgive me if I slugged her on the day of Carrie's funeral. I'm gonna sneak out the back door."

Patches comes running, and we trudge past the feed barn, the chicken house, and the pigpen. Bending over, I pick up a stick. I throw it and Patches brings it back. I throw it again and again as we make our way to the creek.

I follow the water to its narrowest point and jump across. Patches follows, and we head toward Tom and Frank's fishing shack.

After pushing the door closed behind me, I dust off a chair and have a seat. Patches cuddles up at my feet. "I couldn't stand being around Liza Phillips another minute," I tell him.

Patches whimpers in response. I swear my dog understands more than most people. My eyes feel heavy, and I let them drift shut.

"Jessie, Jessie Pearl. Are you in there?"

I pull my coat around me, convinced that I'm dreaming, but then J.T. charges in. "What'd you run off for?"

I bend down and give Patches a hug. "Because the house was too hot and crowded. All the commotion was getting on my nerves."

J.T. walks over and pulls me to my feet. "I've got a present for you," he says, reaching into his coat pocket.

I tear into the brown paper wrapping and find a red velvet ribbon. "It's awfully pretty," I say. "But why'd you buy me a present?"

J.T. bends down and kisses my lips lightly. "Because your fifteenth birthday was last month and I missed it."

Looping my arms around his neck, I kiss him back. "With Carrie being so sick, we didn't celebrate my birthday."

J.T. gives me that lazy smile of his. "Last Christmas was the only time I've ever seen your hair down. I remember thinkin' it looked pretty, and that you needed a red ribbon to match your dress."

I tilt my head back and look into his eyes. "I feel sick inside. Like I won't ever be happy again."

"You'll be happy again," J.T. says. "I'll see to that."

I rest my head on his chest, thinking back to the morning Ky was born. How I knew a baby would tie Carrie down and how glad I was to still be free. "J.T.," I whisper, "I'm gonna have to give up my dream of being a teacher to look after Ky. I'm scared. I don't even know how to take care of a baby."

"You'll learn," he says.

13 | THANKSGIVING

"Thanksgiving is hard when you're not feeling thankful," I say.

Maude crams a handful of stuffing into the turkey's carcass.
"You're right about that," she says, "and Christmas will be worse yet."

I slice several peeled potatoes into a pot. "I wish Carrie were
here."

"We all do," Maude says, "but there ain't no help for it." She
finishes stuffing the turkey and washes her hands. "I canned a lot
of vegetables over the summer. At least you won't go hungry when I
leave."

I take the dipper and cover the potatoes with water. "You aren't
planning to go anytime soon, are you?"

Maude nods. "Yes, Jessie, I am. My no-account son-in-law is
coming to get me tomorrow."

"Tomorrow!" Water sloshes out of the dipper and onto the floor.
"Don't go," I beg. "We need you here. I've never looked after a baby
for longer than an afternoon."

Maude pulls a handkerchief from her apron pocket and wipes
her eyes. "It feels good to be needed," she says. "But my daughter is
expectin' again, and I'd best get home." She tilts my chin and looks
into my eyes. "Don't sell yourself short, Jessie. It won't be easy, but
you'll do just fine."

I bend over and wipe up the spill. I'd keep begging her if it would
do any good.

"Anna and Cole are in the parlor," Maude says. "I'll keep an eye
on dinner. Why don't you run and play with the little ones?"

Anna's cheeks are flushed from the cold, and she's holding an apple
pie. "Happy Thanksgiving," she says. "Something sure smells good."

"It's Maude's stuffing," I say. "Sage is her secret ingredient."

Vivi runs over and hugs me around the knees. When I lift her
up, her short arms circle my neck. "Vivi needs a ride," she says.

I settle into the rocker for a game of straddle-a-stump. "Again," Vivi cries when it's over.

Pa claps Cole on the back. "Good to see you. What's in that bag you're holdin'?"

"Ky's clothes," he says. "Frank asked us to bring them."

It feels like my old life is being swept away by a fast river current. Tomorrow I'll be a mother. My eyes are drawn to Frank and Ky on the settee. Ky stares back at me with Carrie's solemn blue eyes.

The sputter and spit of Tom's old car gives me an excuse to leave the room. I set Vivi down and escape to the porch. "Hey, Jessie, we need some help," Tom calls.

I step carefully across the ice-crusted grass. Tom hands me a sweet potato pie before helping Sophie from the passenger side. Lord! She is plumper than our Thanksgiving turkey!

"I saw that look!" Sophie says. "Not one word about the size of my stomach. I'm liable to punch the first person who mentions it!"

In the kitchen Anna is adding another pat of butter to the potatoes. "I bet J.T. is coming for dinner," she teases when she sees me.

I place Sophie's sweet potato pie on the counter. "What makes you think that?"

Maude snorts. "It ain't hard to figure out. Why else would you be wearin' a dress?"

I feel my face flush. "He's having dinner at home, but he's stopping by later for pie and coffee."

Maude pours the gravy into a bowl. "I wasn't born yesterday. That boy ain't one bit interested in coffee. He's hopin' for pie and kisses."

Anna laughs so hard her eyes water.

"Why are you laughin'?" Maude asks. "I'm just tellin' the truth."

I glare at both of them.

Maude takes off her apron and winks at me. "Jessie, call everybody to dinner. It took me all day to cook it, but it won't take this crowd more than twenty minutes to eat it. Don't that beat all?"

Pa takes his place at the head of the table.

"Dear Lord, thank you for a roof over our heads, food on the table, and a new baby on the way. I know you won't mind me sayin' that our hearts are heavy this year. We're trustin' you for better times ahead and to comfort all of us who miss Carrie. Amen."

"Amen," Frank echoes.

Anna and Sophie both have tears flowing. Vivi reaches over and pats Anna's arm. "Don't cry, Mama."

Anna tugs on one of Vivi's curls. "Don't worry, little one. I'll be just fine." Anna wipes her eyes on her napkin. "Enough," she says. "We're scaring Vivi and turning Thanksgiving into a day of mourning. Jessie, pass the potatoes."

I take a spoonful and scoop some on Frank's plate too. "You'd best eat up," I tell him. "Maude is going home tomorrow, and you know what that means."

Frank's eyes bulge out of their sockets. "Say it ain't so," he says. "How are we gonna survive on Jessie's cookin'?"

Tom laughs. "Jessie's pound cakes taste good, but they always turn out lopsided. I never could figure out why."

Anna spears a turkey thigh and passes the platter. "It's because Jessie's in too big of a hurry. She doesn't even out the batter before she bakes the cake."

Everybody has a funny story about my cooking except for Cole. He leans toward me. "Does all this teasin' hurt your feelings, Jessie?"

He may be the size of Paul Bunyan, but he's got a marshmallow heart. "No, Cole, I don't mind. Better to laugh at me than cry about the empty places at the table."

Anna is the first one to push her plate away.

"Cole," I say, "Anna didn't eat very much. Is she feeling okay?"

He scrunches up his forehead. "She caught a cold after Carrie's funeral and can't seem to get rid of it. I'll ask my sister to visit for a few days so that Anna can rest."

While we're washing up, J.T. moseys around to the back door.

Anna smiles at me. "Take your beau for a walk. We'll finish up here."

I snatch my coat from a peg near the door. "Be back in an hour for pie and coffee," Maude calls.

14 | KY

Anna pulls on her coat and takes Ky in her arms. "I'll miss you, little man. Be good for your aunt Jessie." She kisses the top of his head and hands him to me.

Ky struggles in my arms, reaching for Anna. "Mamamama!" he screams. "Mamama." Big tears plop down his chubby cheeks.

Frank reaches over and tickles Ky's tummy. Frank makes silly faces, sticking out his tongue and pulling on Ky's ears, but it doesn't help.

"Mama!" Ky shrieks.

"I could keep him for a while longer," Anna says.

Frank shakes his head. "I appreciate the offer, but that'll only make it harder. It's time he came home."

Tears spill onto Anna's cheeks. "Frank, I love him like he was my own. If you ever need my help again, just ask."

She scoops Vivi into her arms, and Cole holds the door for them. "She'll be okay," he says. "It's just hard for her to give him up."

As Pa and Frank are finishing breakfast, Ky starts to cry. I was hoping to get the dishes washed before he woke up, but no such luck.

"I'll see to him," Frank says. "Go ahead with your chores."

I put some water on to boil and plug the sink.

"Jessie," Frank yells from his room, "come quick!"

Pa takes a last sip of coffee. "I'll fill up the sink," he says. "Go see what's got Frank in such a panic."

I race down the hall and slide to a stop in front of Frank's room. "What happened?" I ask.

Frank's mouth hangs open wide enough to stick an apple inside. "Ky's poop was runny, and he started kicking like a mule. Before I could stop him, we were both filthy, and it was runnin' down the wall."

I giggle.

"Jessie, it ain't one bit funny. I'll have to change my shirt."

I laugh until tears run down my cheeks, then take a cloth from the bedside table. Holding Ky's feet in one hand, I clean his legs and bottom with the other. "Always hold his feet," I say to Frank. "Anna taught me that. Do you want to feed him breakfast, or clean the walls and wash his stinky diapers?"

"I was plannin' to chop wood," Frank says. "Colder weather is comin', and the woodpile's low."

It's just like a man to make a mess and expect a woman to clean it up. "I'll handle it," I tell him. "But don't look for dinner to be on time."

Anna finds me out back by the rock furnace. "I see you're making stink soup," she says.

I give Ky's diapers a stir with the sassafras stick. "I love having company, but what are you doing out in the cold? Where's Vivi?"

Anna smiles at me. "Cole's sister is staying with us for a few weeks, and she's watching Vivi. I thought a walk might do me good, and I wanted to check on Ky."

"He's napping," I say. "Thank the Good Lord he can't climb out of the crib yet."

"Those days are coming fast," Anna says. "It's hard when a child can walk but doesn't understand danger. You'll have to watch him every second."

"It can't be any harder than taking care of Carrie."

I rinse the diapers, and Anna helps me wring them out. "I'll hang these by the stove to dry," she says. "Don't worry, Jessie. I'll help you all I can."

While I'm folding diapers, the first snowflakes of winter fall. Ky has never seen snow before. I hold him up to the window, and he presses his palms against the glass. He reaches for the snowflakes as if he's trying to catch them. His eyes widen and he laughs. I hug him close, smiling at how happy he sounds.

15 | 'TIS THE SEASON

"Christmas Eve is my favorite night of the year," I say.

Frank stands just inside Ky's nursery. Now that we've painted it blue and moved in the crib and rocking chair, all traces of Carrie's sickroom are gone. "Mine too," he says.

I push Ky's arms through the navy-and-white-checked romper Anna made for him.

"He's a handsome little fellow," Frank says.

I grin at him. "You conceited oaf, he's the spitting image of you."

Frank stares at Ky's face. "Not quite. He has Carrie's blue eyes. I see her every time I look at him."

"Jessie," Pa calls. "The water is ready for your bath."

I thrust Ky into Frank's arms. "Take care of your son. I've got some primping to do."

Steam rises from the large tin tub Pa has pulled into the kitchen. I stick my fingers in to make sure the water is just right, shuck my clothes, and climb in. I stretch like a cat until the water nearly reaches my chin. I let it wash away the week's dirt and grime.

Pa knocks on the kitchen door. "Jessie, have you fallen asleep in the tub again? Me and Frank still need a bath."

"Almost finished," I call. I give my hair a final rinse, then step out, wrap myself in a towel, and scamper across the cracked linoleum floor. "All done," I holler.

Alone in my room, I drag a comb through my waist-length hair. When it's free of tangles, I put on my underclothes and the red dress that J.T. liked last Christmas. It's a little tighter across the bodice.

While my hair dries, I dream of Carrie playing "Silent Night" on her dulcimer. I miss her singing most of all. It brought magic to our house.

"Jessie," Frank calls. "I'm going out to crank the car."

I tie J.T.'s red velvet ribbon in my hair. "I'll be right there," I yell. On my way out, I slip my present for him into my coat pocket.

Going to church at night has a special feeling to it. Oil lamps softly light our sanctuary. Neighbors speak in hushed tones. I pause for a minute and soak up the wonder of it before taking my place on the hard-backed pew. "Tom and Sophie aren't coming," Anna whispers. "The baby is due any time now."

Thanks to Anna's sewing, we all have nice church clothes. Vivi looks like she stepped out of the Sears and Roebuck catalogue in her red plaid dress. Cole tips his head in my direction and smiles. "Ky's romper is a perfect fit," I tell Anna. Her face lights up at the sight of him perched on Frank's lap.

My eyes scan the crowd, searching for J.T. He's sitting close to the front with his parents. My heart aches at how handsome he looks in his dark serge suit. He's the only Christmas present I need.

"Welcome," Preacher White says. The way his face shines from the kerosene lamps reminds me of Moses and the burning bush. "Turn with me," he says, "to the Christmas story in Luke's gospel.

"*And Joseph also went up from Galilee, out of the city of Nazareth, into Judaea, to the city of David, which is called Bethlehem, because he was of the house and family of David.*"

Preacher White pauses, and Abe and Bett Bowman play "O Little Town of Bethlehem" on their fiddles. A young girl dressed as Mary and a little boy dressed as Joseph step forward and kneel by the manger.

"*And she brought forth her firstborn son; and she wrapped him in swaddling clothes, and laid him in a manger, because there was no room for them in the inn.*"

Bett and Abe take up their fiddles again, and I hum along to "Away in a Manger."

The shepherds walk down the aisle to join Mary and Joseph. They bow their heads to worship the Christ child. The smallest shepherd starts wiggling. He hops from one foot to the other. I'm not sure if he's tired of standing or if he needs to pee. I hear muffled laughter from the pews. Eli squirms some more, drops his shepherd staff, and runs to Pansy. She shrugs and pulls him into her lap. Pa chuckles, and I'm grateful to the smallest Pilcher boy. Pa doesn't laugh nearly enough since Ma and Carrie died.

My favorite carol plays near the end. "*Joy to the world,*" we sing, "*the

Lord is come! Let earth receive her king." The music is so uplifting that for just a minute I forget to be sad.

"Let's bow our heads for the closing prayer," Preacher White says. When he finishes, I follow Anna and Cole to the tall cedar tree trimmed with popcorn and oranges.

J.T. makes his way toward me, parting our neighbors like Moses did the Red Sea. "Evening, Jessie. How about a cup of cider?"

I nod and follow him to the back room where refreshments are served. "Joseph," Liza says, "would you like some lemon pound cake? I made it especially for you."

He smiles at her. "That's mighty nice of you, Liza. Could you put two slices on a plate? One for me and one for Jessie."

I pour two mugs of cider and give her a sweet smile. I swear that Liza hisses just like a snake.

J.T. leads the way outdoors to the back steps. "I know it's cold, but I wanted a few minutes alone with you," he says.

We carefully balance our cake and cider and sit down on the steps. He reaches into his coat pocket. "I made you a present," he says.

I tear into the brown paper wrapping and lift out a delicately carved box. A jewelry box, but I don't own anything fancy.

"Do you have any use for it?" J.T. asks, and his voice wobbles.

I smile at how unsure he sounds. I think it shows how much he wants to please me. "It's going to be my memory box."

He lets out a deep breath. "Good! That's real good. What will you put in there?"

I touch my hair. "My birthday ribbon, Carrie's letter, a photograph of my sisters, and a lock of Ky's hair. All the most important things."

J.T. looks around and then gives me a quick kiss. "It sounds more like a treasure box," he says.

I reach into my coat pocket. "I have something for you too."

He rips into his present and strokes the soft yarn. I stare at his hands. "Jessie, did you make this scarf yourself?"

I nod. "I did, and it took me nearly a year. You know how I can't stand to sit still."

J.T. laughs as I take the scarf from him and wind it around his neck. "That tickles," he says. "Thank you, Jessie. It'll keep me warm this winter."

"You're welcome. Would you like to stop by tomorrow for cocoa and Christmas cookies?"

J.T.'s eyebrows shoot up. "Did you bake the cookies?"

I lightly punch his arm. "Hey, my cooking has improved."

"I'll be the judge of that," he says. He grins and helps me to my feet. "Come on, we'd best go back inside before they send out a search party."

I pick up the plates, then follow J.T. At the top of the steps I turn around and look in the direction of the cemetery.

When I was a little girl, Ma always made pancakes and sausage patties for Christmas breakfast. Serving them reminds me of happier times. "I believe Ky has his mama's sweet tooth," Frank says.

Ky rules like a little prince from his high chair, stuffing bite-sized pieces of pancake into his mouth. He eats first from one hand, then from the other.

"I love watchin' him," Pa says. "Ain't nothin' funnier than watchin' a baby."

I hold up my hand for everybody to pipe down. "I think I hear a car."

Frank pushes away from the table. "I wonder who's out this early? I'll see who it is."

I scrape my plate with my fork for the last bit of syrup.

"Jessie," Frank calls. "Cook up some more pancakes. Doc's starvin'."

Doc follows Frank into the kitchen and claps Pa on the back. "It's time I delivered some good news to this family," he says. "Tom and Sophie have a girl!"

I smile until I notice the tears pooling in Frank's eyes. They remind me of the morning Ky was born.

I walk over and give Frank a hug. "I'm thinking about her too," I whisper.

 | 1923 |

16 | SNOW SLEDDING

Pa picks up a block of wood and starts to whittle by the parlor stove. "There's a heap of snow outside," he says, "and it's still comin' down." Frank leans in the doorway with his arms crossed. "Ky will probably nap for a couple of hours. Why don't you read to us, Jessie?" His favorite book is *The Adventures of Tom Sawyer*. I borrowed it from Sophie, and we all love it so much that she let me keep it.

Pa sets his chair to rocking. "Boy, that Tom and Huck are full of the devil. Both of 'em need a good trip to the woodshed. Go on, Jessie. I love the way you read a story. Reminds me of your ma."

I thumb through the book to Chapter 13 and read about the boys sailing on a raft to Jackson's Island. About the time my voice is giving out, J.T. stops by for a visit.

He follows Frank into the parlor and smiles at me. "If you can tear yourself away from that book, I'll take you sledding. I borrowed Earl's Flexible Flyer."

Pa looks up from his whittling. "Go have fun, Jessie. The fresh air will do you good."

J.T. pulls the sled with his left hand and holds mine with his right. My fingers tingle, even through our mittens. I wonder if he feels it too. "Do you want to sled on the hill behind Anna's house or the one past the fishing shack?" I ask him.

J.T. gives me a mischievous smile. "Past the fishing shack," he says. We walk in silence, with the snow peppering our faces. I suck in my breath, savoring these feelings like a cup of hot cocoa.

When we reach the fishing shack, J.T. stops, hoping we'll go inside. I give his hand a squeeze. "Sledding first."

He smiles at me. "Okay, sledding first, but you can't blame a guy for hopin'." J.T. bends down and kisses the tip of my nose.

I laugh, then drop his hand and race through the snow to our favorite sledding spot.

When he catches up, I give him a playful shove. "I want to go first."

J.T. crosses his arms and nods. "Let's see if you can still sled as good as I can or if you've turned into a sissy."

I get a running start beside the sled, belly flop onto the wooden slats, and speed down the hill. "Woohoooo! Woohooo!"

J.T. claps as I drag the sled back up. "That's my girl!" he says, and when I bend over to catch my breath, he lobs a snowball at my shoulder.

I laugh, scoop up a handful of powder, and pelt him back.

"Truce," J.T. calls. "Truce! I want a turn on the sled." He takes off running and does his own belly flop. Racing like a bullet, the sled veers off course and into the woods. J.T.'s body launches from the sled and rolls over. He tumbles again and again before landing face down in the snow.

"J.T.! J.T.!" I scream as I lurch through the drifts to the bottom of the hill. Kneeling beside him, I touch the back of his head. "J.T., talk to me. Please talk to me," I beg.

He flips over onto his back and pulls me on top of him. "I was just kiddin' around," he says.

I take his face between my hands and kiss him so hard my toes curl. "Don't ever scare me like that again," I say.

J.T. smiles at me. "I pulled that stunt on you once before when we were kids."

"I remember, but now it's different. I'm afraid of bad things happening to the people I care about."

"Does that mean you care about me, Jessie?"

I scramble to my feet like a spooked mare and grab the sled. "Race you to the top of the hill," I call.

17 | KY'S BIG DAY

Ky's screams echo from his crib throughout the whole house. I try harder to ignore him. If he doesn't take a nap, I'll never get his birthday cake in the oven.

Carrie's gentle voice plays inside my head. *Jessie, rock him to sleep, and then make the cake.*

"You're right," I whisper, but she doesn't answer. That's how it happens, little bits of advice when I least expect it, and then she's gone.

J.T. says it's probably my imagination. That I miss Carrie so badly, I actually hear her voice. But Anna and I know different. She hears Carrie too.

I wash the flour from my hands and hurry to Ky's room. "Don't cry, sweet boy. Aunt Jessie will rock you to sleep."

Settling in the rocking chair, Ky and I both relax. I pat his back and remember the morning he was born. So many things have changed in the past year that I can hardly believe it.

While Ky naps, I slide his cake into the oven. Now for the rest of the meal. Ma always made chicken pie for our birthday suppers. I've never tried one before, but I'm determined to keep up her traditions.

After mixing flour and salt, I work the lard in with my hands. So far, so good. I add cold water and press the dough into a ball. If Ma were here, she'd chill the dough for about an hour on the back porch. I don't have that kind of time. Ky will wake up any minute now. He may be adorable, but patience is not one of his virtues.

I grab the rolling pin and attack the dough. When it's too sticky, I add more flour. There, that's better. I take up the rolling pin again. Now there are holes in the crust. I've rolled it too thin.

Holy crow! There's no reason to make myself crazy. I cut the dough into squares and throw it into the broth. Chicken and dumplings will be plenty good enough.

———

"Jessie," Anna says, "dinner is delicious. You got the dumplings just right."

As I smile at Anna, Frank nudges my leg underneath the table and gives me that knowing grin. I kick him back and ask Pa to pass the green beans.

"Too bad Tom and Sophie couldn't be here," Frank says.

Anna takes a sip of water. "Sophie doesn't want to bring the baby out into the cold. She's real cautious because of what happened to Violet."

"Understandable," Cole says. "I'm sure we'd feel the same way."

Vivi points at Ky. "Look! He's a messy baby."

Pa chuckles. "Ky has more dumplings in his hair than made it to his mouth."

Frank looks over at me for direction. "Would you like me to clean him up, Jessie?"

I shake my head. "Why bother? Wait until he has his cake."

Anna helps me clear the table and starts the coffee. "Jessie," she says, "this cake is—perfect! It's not one bit lopsided!"

I laugh at the stunned look on her face. "Let me tell you a secret. I used to make them lopsided on purpose. Ma would shake her head and mix up extra icing to build up the low part. I'd always cut my piece from the side loaded with icing."

Anna claps her hands and laughs. "You always gave Ma fits, Jessie."

While we visit in the parlor, Ky grabs hold of Anna's chair and pulls himself up. "He'll be walking before long," she says.

Frank smiles down at his son. "If I'm holdin' on to him, he can already take a few steps. But he's still afraid to try it on his own."

Vivi plops down in the middle of the floor and holds out her arms. "C'mere, Ky." He shakes his head and hides against Anna's skirt. Vivi keeps pleading, "C'mere, baby." Finally he lets go of the chair, takes two steps, and lands on his bottom. He crawls back over and pulls himself up again.

"Look at that," Pa says. His joints creak when he gets on his knees. "Dang if Ky ain't walkin'."

The rest of us scramble to the floor like Pa. Sitting in a circle, we hold out our hands. "C'mon, Ky. You can do it!" I tell him. He crawls to me, and I help him onto his feet. When he's steady, I turn him like a wind-up toy toward Frank.

Frank gives him a hug and points to Pa. "Go see Grandpa."

Pa sends him toddling to Anna. Vivi crosses her arms. She pushes her lips out in a mad pout.

I hustle to my feet. "Come on, Vivi. I've got a surprise for you." I take her to my room and brush her blond curls. When they're tangle-free and framing her face, I tie a blue ribbon in her hair. "Oh, Vivi, you look beautiful! Girls have the prettiest hair."

She reaches up and touches the ribbon. "Let me see."

While Vivi admires herself, I catch Anna's reflection in the mirror as she walks in from the hallway. "Thank you for being so sweet to her," she says. "I guess Vivi is jealous of all the attention Ky's receiving."

I shrug. "She probably feels left out. I used to be jealous of you and Carrie. Especially when you'd talk about things I was too young to understand."

Anna moves over and wraps her arms around Vivi and me. "I never loved Carrie more than you," she says. "I just loved you differently."

That makes perfect sense to me. It's how I feel about Vivi and Ky.

Vivi squirms and breaks our three-way hug. "You didn't fix my lips," she says. I rub some Rosebud Salve on them and Anna laughs.

"My daughter is all girl," she says. She bends down and takes Vivi's hand. "Jessie, would you mind if we left a little early? I'm feeling awfully tired."

"No," I say. "I wouldn't mind at all. You do look tired."

Anna touches her stomach. "Maybe it's another baby."

"I hope so. We could sure use some good news."

18 | VINEY

Viney stops by on a chilly February afternoon. "Thought I'd pay you a visit," she says. "After we start the plant beds next week, I won't have much spare time."

Jostling Ky on my hip, I throw my free arm around her shoulder. "Come in, Viney. I'm glad to see you."

I lead the way to the kitchen. "Would you like some milk and sugar cookies?"

Viney gives me a suspicious look. "Did *you* bake the cookies?"

I stick my tongue out at her. "Afraid I'll poison you? Don't worry. Anna did the baking."

I put Ky in his high chair, and he bangs the tray with his fists. While I pour him a cup of milk, Viney sits down at the kitchen table and helps herself. "Last year I was in such an all-fired hurry to graduate," she says, "but it's been a lonely winter without school."

"At least you got to finish," I say.

Viney looks away from me and down at her cookie. "I'm sorry, Jessie. I know how you wanted to be a teacher. It must have been hard when the rest of us graduated without you."

I shrug, not wanting pity, and take a seat across from her. "It can't be helped. I'm needed at home." Tears well up in my eyes and I brush them away. "So tell me all the news. I missed church because Ky had a cold."

Viney blushes and then gives me a happy smile. "I know you don't like Liza Phillips, but I'm sweet on her brother, Earl."

Ky bangs his fist, demanding another cookie. While I break one in two, I say, "There's nothing wrong with Earl. He's J.T.'s best friend. It's Liza that gets on my last nerve."

"That Liza can be a witch all right," Viney says, and then her voice drops to a whisper. "Earl is a good kisser."

I smile at her and whisper back, "So is J.T."

Viney looks down at the table. "Jessie, when was the last time you saw J.T.?"

"About two weeks ago. Why?"

"Because he and Earl are talking again about moving to Winston."

I tug on the end of my braid. "That's just talk," I say. "J.T. wouldn't really leave. Not after telling Pa he wants to marry me someday."

Viney squeals. "Marry? Are you ready for that?"

I push the plate of cookies over so that she can have another one. "Of course not. I want to be a teacher first, but with Ky to take care of, I don't see how that can ever happen." I turn and gaze out the window. "Viney, when J.T. kisses me, college is the last thing on my mind."

She laughs. "I know what you mean." She looks around the kitchen with raised eyebrows. I still haven't washed the dinner dishes. "How are you doing?" she asks. "With the house and taking care of Ky?"

I push back my chair and pace across the floor. "I love Ky, but I have to watch him every minute since he started walking." I point to the sink full of dishes. "The house is not as clean as Ma or Carrie kept it, but the men don't seem to mind."

Viney sips her milk. "What else?" she asks. "I've known you for a long time, and I can tell when you're unhappy."

Tears gather and threaten to spill over. "I'm afraid. Afraid every day for the rest of my life will be just like this one: scrubbing, cooking, cleaning. I'll never see the ocean or the mountains. Nothing special will ever happen to me."

Viney nods. "Would that really be so terrible, Jessie? Think of how much you love J.T." She stands and lifts Ky from his high chair. "You're just feeling restless again." She brushes crumbs from his shirt. "I'll play with Ky for a while. It'll give you a chance to catch up on the housework."

I plug the sink and put on a kettle of water. "Your visit is just what I needed. You're a true friend, Viney Brown."

While the men plant the tobacco seeds, I bundle Ky in his winter coat, hat, and mittens. I carry him on my hip to the garden behind the house. "Aunt Jessie needs to plant the peas," I say. "Be a good boy."

I reach into my pocket and give Ky some of the animals that Pa carved for him. He loves the puppy dog the most. "Sit right here," I say, "and play with the animals."

Keeping my eye on him, I dig into the red clay soil. I plant the peas about an inch deep and two inches apart. "Moooo," Ky says, holding up his cow.

"Moo, moo," I call back. He's not talking yet, but I've taught him most of the animal sounds.

I plant a few more peas and look up. "No!" I yell, and race over to Ky. "Put that stick down," I tell him, "before you poke your eyes out."

He points toward the woods beyond the garden. "Rabbit," I say. "Baby rabbit." Ky gives me a toothless smile, and I kiss both his chubby cheeks. Watching him reminds me of Carrie's letter. *Before I was sick, I didn't take enough time to enjoy the wonder that was all around me.*

I take a break from planting and sit on the cold ground beside Ky. He climbs into my lap and points toward the sky. I kiss the top of his head, breathing in the sweet baby smell of him.

19 | TROUBLE

March winds nearly blow me away on the road to Anna's house. Bouncing Ky on my hip, I step into her cold kitchen. Crumbs and dirty footprints tell me she's having a bad day.

"Hey, what's going on here?" I joke. "Your kitchen is in worse shape than mine."

Anna rocks in a chair by the kitchen stove. She runs her hand through her uncombed hair. "I don't know what's wrong with me," she says. She picks up a shirt from the mending that lies untouched at her feet. "I don't have any energy. Since Carrie died, I'm just not myself."

"Where is Vivi?"

"I asked Cole to take her to his sister's house until I feel better."

"Anna," I say, "go to bed. If Ma were here, that's what she'd tell you to do."

Anna shakes her head. "I'm not really sick. Just sad because of Carrie."

I rock Ky on my hip. "Would it be all right if he takes a nap in your guest room? That way we can have a nice talk."

Anna nods, and I carry Ky down the hall. I lift him over the rails of Vivi's old crib. "Nap time," I say, and kiss the top of his head. He reaches for me like a prisoner through the bars of his jail cell. For the first time ever, I ignore him. "Sorry, sweet boy, you have to stay here."

I hurry back to the kitchen and kneel in front of Anna. "Go to bed," I repeat. "I'll clean the kitchen and make supper. When Cole comes home, I'm sending him for Doc Benbow."

Anna looks at me with panic in her eyes and clutches both my arms. "I don't need to see Doc, you hear? Let me rest for a few minutes, and then I'll be on my feet again."

I want to believe her. I want a good nap to fix everything. "Let me make you a cup of tea," I say, "and after Cole gets home, we'll decide what to do."

Chores make waiting for Cole more bearable. I wipe the kitchen counters and mop the floor.

Anna has several potatoes lying in a basket, and I peel them for potato soup. I add a chopped onion and a little parsley to the pot. At last I hear Cole's heavy footsteps on the porch.

"Mm, something smells good!" he says, slamming the door behind him. "Hey, Jessie. Where is Anna?"

"She's resting."

He takes a seat and rubs his forehead. "The sawmill has been extra busy. We've got a big order from one of the furniture companies in High Point."

No wonder Cole's tuckered out. I'm sorry as can be about adding to his troubles. "I know you've got a lot on your mind," I say, "but Anna's sick."

His eyelids droop. "I know she's tired. We both are. Carrie's death has been hard on the whole family."

I remember Carrie's letter: *Sometimes men have a way of not noticing all the details.* "No, Cole. I think it's more than that. She needs to see Doc Benbow."

Cole's eyebrows knit together. "Anna just needs to rest."

The tension inside of me builds when Ky wakes up, screaming like a panther. "I have to feed and change the baby," I say. "Don't argue with me. Crank the car and leave. *Now*."

Frank finds me pacing with Ky on my hip. "I figured you were either here or at Tom's. Dang it, Jessie, stand still and tell me what's wrong."

"Anna's sick," I tell him. "Cole's gone for the doctor."

Frank holds his arms out and takes Ky from me. "What do you think is wrong with her?" he asks.

I shake my head and look at the floor.

"Damn it!" Frank says. "It can't be."

I grab hold of his arm. "Don't go borrowing trouble. Take Ky home so Pa won't worry. Doc can give me a ride when he's finished."

Frank hugs his son tight. "She breastfed Ky for months," he says. "What if…"

I squeeze his arm harder. "Don't say it. You hear me? Just take Ky and go."

Anna is awake when I peek in the bedroom door. I pull a chair beside the bed and take her hand. "I asked Cole to fetch Doc Benbow."

She looks back at me, letting out a weary sigh. "I already know what's wrong, Jessie, and so do you."

Tears sting my eyes. "Ma lied!" I say fiercely. "She promised that God would never give us more troubles than we could handle."

Anna closes her eyes. "Ma didn't lie, Jessie. I believe that."

Her breathing sounds heavy, and she drifts off to sleep. I keep watch over her. *Help us*, I beg Ma. *Please help us.*

I walk over and lean my head against the windowpane.

While Doc examines Anna, I ladle potato soup into a bowl. "Sit, Cole. My cooking is not as good as Anna's, but it won't kill you."

He follows my orders like a child and spoons soup into his mouth. "It's good, Jessie. Your cookin' is a lot better than it used to be."

I put on a pot of coffee, hearing Carrie's voice inside my head. *Eat*, she tells me. *Keep up your strength because Ky needs you.*

I finish my soup, then pour coffee and wash the bowls. "What is taking so danged long?" I ask.

Cole's big shoulders shake, and he hides his face in his hands. He already knows what's wrong, same as I do.

I hear Doc's footsteps and brace myself for bad news. He walks into the kitchen and pats Cole's back. "I listened to Anna's lungs, and it's very likely she has tuberculosis."

I nod to show Doc I understand. Just like with Carrie, he has to examine her sputum under a microscope.

Cole doesn't look up, but his sobs sound like a wounded animal. Doc sits down in the chair facing him. "Cole, you have to pull yourself together. Anna needs you." Doc keeps murmuring to Cole in a calm, steady voice. I don't know how he can deal with so much suffering.

Finally Doc turns to look at me. "Jessie," he says. "Why don't you go have a visit with Anna? She wants to tell you about her decision."

Anna is sitting up in bed combing her hair. "Doc told you," she says matter-of-factly.

I nod. "Yes, he did. Cole is taking it pretty hard."

Anna places the comb on her bedside table, and her expression grows tender. "I hate hurting him. That's the main reason I didn't face the truth sooner."

She motions for me to sit down, acting bossy, more like her usual self. "Talking to Doc was like a shot of hope," she says. "I'm not recovering from childbirth like Carrie, and I've been diagnosed sooner."

I grip the chair bottom with both hands and close my eyes. "Thank God," I say.

Anna reaches out and rubs my bowed head. "Jessie, I'm going away. Doc says my best chance at recovery is in a sanatorium."

"But Carrie said..."

"I know what Carrie said," Anna continues. "She made her decision, and I'm making a different one."

Anna's bottom lip trembles, and I can feel mine trembling too. "What about Vivi?" I ask. "Do you want me to look after her?"

Anna shakes her head. "Jessie, you're a strong young woman, but you can't manage two households and two small children. I think Maude is the answer."

I squint and pucker my lips like Maude. "You'll have the cleanest house in the county. And Vivi will be the best-behaved girl you ever saw. House cleanin' and raisin' children are two of my talents."

Anna laughs at me. "Carrie told you a long time ago to quit imitating Maude. Your face is going to freeze in a Maude-like pucker."

At the mention of Carrie's name, the hairs on the back of my neck stand up. Sometimes when Anna and I are alone it feels like Carrie is close by. "What do you want me to do?" I ask.

Anna feels it too. She speaks just above a whisper, squeezing my hand. "Watch over Vivi," she says. "Maude will make sure she's clean and fed, but I need you to read her fairytales, make sure she has ribbons for her hair, and let her splash in the creek."

I stare into Anna's eyes. "I promise. I promise to do all of those things."

Anna loosens her grip on my hand. "I need to give you something," she says. "A book. It's in my cedar chest, there at the foot of the bed."

I walk over and lift the lid. I find a journal nestled among the quilts and embroidery. "I wrote down Ma's recipes," Anna says. "And home remedies too. Ma got them from her mother."

I flip through the book and see Ma's recipes for pickled beets, vinegar pickles, chicken pie, egg custard, and lots of other dishes. "Toward the back," Anna says. "That's where the home remedies are."

I turn to them, read a few, and laugh. "Here's a funny one: 'Place your shoes upside down under your bed to keep from having cramps.'"

Anna laughs with me. "Some of them are silly, but lots of them do work. Especially the teas."

I clutch the journal to my chest, knowing what it means. I'm the keeper of family traditions now. "I'm scared," I whisper.

"Me too," Anna says. "But don't tell Cole. It will only make it worse for him."

She's leaving. I don't see how it can get any worse.

Cole raps his knuckles against the open door. "Can I come in?" he asks.

"Of course you can," Anna answers. She holds out her arms to comfort him. I take the journal and go.

21 | GOODBYES

I pack a knitted cap and five pairs of wool socks on top of Anna's sweaters. "Geez, Anna, you're going to Asheville, not the North Pole."

She rocks back and forth in her bedroom chair. "Doc says it's chilly in the mountains. And I'll be sleeping on a screened porch. Plenty of fresh air is part of the cure."

"That's probably why I haven't gotten sick. I spend a lot of time outdoors." Next I fold her heavy coat and mittens. "It's only April. Surely you'll be home before winter."

Anna shakes her head. "Probably not. Doc told me to plan on being away for at least a year."

My throat clogs up so that I have to whisper. "A whole year? That seems like such a long time."

"Don't look so sad," Anna says. "I'll write to you every day, since I won't be allowed to do much else."

According to Doc, Anna will be lying in bed nearly all the time to rest her lungs.

I hear the heavy clomp of Maude's shoes, and then she sticks her head in the door. "I fixed ham biscuits and pound cake for your trip."

"That sounds good," Anna says. "Cole will appreciate it."

Anna moves around the sitting room, touching each piece of furniture. Her voice sounds steady, but the slight tremor in her hands tells me different. "I've never spent a night away from home," she says. "No tears from any of you or I'll cry too."

It's too late for that. Sophie is already dabbing at her eyes with a handkerchief. Tom puts his arm around her shoulders. "Don't," he says. "It'll be harder for Anna if we all blubber like babies."

Frank looks down at the floor. He already told me he thinks Anna will die in the sanatorium. I think his sadness is more complicated: he wonders if going away might have saved Carrie. I wonder the same thing.

Pa steps forward and wraps his arms around Anna. "Take good care of yourself," he says gruffly. He pats her back, then holds her at arm's length. "Be sure and write," he says. "I won't rest easy until you're back home."

When Pa steps away, Vivi grabs Anna around the knees. "Don't go, Mama."

Anna strokes Vivi's curls, and that's her undoing. "I can't leave her," she sobs. "I just can't."

My jaw clenches. "Yes, you can," I say. "Better to leave for a while than to leave for good." I walk over and tap Vivi on the back. "Vivi, Maude has chocolate pound cake in the kitchen."

"Chocate?" she asks.

"Yep, your favorite!"

Vivi lets go of Anna and gives her a big smile. "Bye, Mama. I want some chocate." When she takes off for the kitchen, Pa follows close behind.

Anna reaches into her pocket for a handkerchief. "Thank you, Jessie."

Maude nods at me and then squeezes Anna's hand. "I'd best supervise the cake cuttin'," she says. "Now don't be worryin' your head about things here. Housekeepin' is one of my talents."

Despite her tears, Anna smiles. "Maude, I feel better just knowing you're in charge." She turns toward Cole. "Saying goodbye is harder than I expected. We'd better go before I change my mind."

Frank and I walk with Anna and Cole to the Model T. I stop beside the car and hand Ky to him. "Your son has turned into a wiggle worm," I say.

While Cole is putting her valise in the back, Anna clutches me to her chest. "Stay close to Vivi," she whispers, "and read Ma's book. There's a lot of wisdom in there, and you never know when you might need it."

"Jessie," J.T. yells. "Where are you, girl?"

I stand up straight, arching my back, and check on Ky. "I'm in the garden," I holler.

J.T. hurries down the path, waving when he sees me. "What are you planting?" he asks.

"Beans, squash, and cucumbers. All the late vegetables."

J.T. reaches into his pocket for a handkerchief and wipes dirt off my cheek. "Jessie Pearl is a beautiful girl," he says. I move closer to him and turn my face up for a kiss.

"That was nice," I say. "I'll take another one."

J.T. grins, but he breaks the hold I have around his neck and walks over to the end of the row. He squats in front of Ky. "What you doin', buddy?"

Ky waves a large kitchen spoon. "Dadadadadada!" he says.

"He's ruining my spoon," I say. "But he loves playing in the dirt. I figure a spoon is a small price to pay to get the garden planted."

J.T. nods. "Seems like a fair trade to me." He tousles Ky's hair, then stands up and looks off toward Pilot Mountain. I get a funny feeling in the pit of my stomach.

"I guess you heard about Anna," I say.

J.T. puts both hands in his pockets. "I'm sorry as can be about that." He stares at the ground, not meeting my eyes.

"Are you afraid of me?" I ask.

J.T. frowns. "Afraid? What do you mean?"

"Afraid that I'm sick like Anna. That I'll give you tuberculosis."

J.T. shakes his head. "No, Jessie, I'm not worried that you're sick. I'm worried you won't understand what I'm about to tell you."

I cross my arms. "Well…just spit it out."

J.T. sighs and taps his foot. "I got a job in Winston," he says. "Me and Earl both did."

Now I feel sick to my stomach, like the first time I had to kill a chicken. "You're leaving me?" I ask.

"It's not like that," J.T. says. "I'm goin' so I can save money. So that I can take care of you someday."

I stomp my foot in the dirt. "Let me tell you how it really is. You're going because you don't want to be a sharecropper like your pa. I didn't enter into your decision. And don't pretend like I did."

J.T. nods. "You're partly right. I don't want to be a sharecropper, but I still want to marry you someday. I shouldn't have to choose."

I give him a sad smile. "You already did. I can't leave here. I promised Carrie that I'd take care of her son."

"But I'll be back," J.T. pleads.

I shake my head. "You can't promise that. Once you're boarding in Winston and have a fancy job, who knows how you'll feel? Who knows what girls you'll meet? Girls who aren't tied to a farm and a baby."

J.T. pulls me into his arms. He kisses me hard and fast. I kiss him back, looping my arms around his neck. Maybe I could make him stay, but he'd be miserable. Always wanting something more.

I push against J.T.'s chest with my hands. "Stop!" I say. "We could go on kissing, but it won't change a thing." I walk over to Ky and put him on my hip. "I hope this job turns out to be everything you want it to be."

J.T. picks up a rock and throws it into the woods. "It doesn't have to be this way," he says. "You could promise to wait for me."

I shake my head. "I'm the one who should be asking for promises, but I can't live my life hoping you'll come back."

J.T.'s hands ball into fists. "Why do you have to make me feel so guilty? If you had the chance to leave for teachers' college, you'd take it."

Ky whimpers and I jostle him on my hip. "Would I? I just don't know anymore. The feelings I have for you tie my heart in knots."

22 | A STUBBORN STREAK

Frank has his dark hair all slicked back, and he smells good too. He leans against the parlor door and says, "Boy, you give up easy."

I slam my book on the settee. Startled at the noise, Ky drops his wooden pig on the floor. I reach down and hand it back to him. "J.T. made his choice," I say. "I don't see any reason why I should be at the going-away party for him and Earl."

Frank shrugs. "May is the perfect time for a get-together. Not too hot or too cold." He uses his most persuasive voice. "Practically everybody we know will be there, but suit yourself. You've got a stubborn streak a mile wide."

I tug on my braid and think about what he said. "Well...what would you do?"

Frank crosses his arms and rocks back on his heels. "If I were you, I'd put on a dress, comb your hair out all pretty and soft, maybe put on a little lipstick too. Show that boy what he'll be missin'."

I give my braid another tug. "Maybe I'll go after all," I say. "But not for J.T. I'm missing Viney, now that I don't see her at school."

Frank laughs. "Go ahead and tell yourself that, but I ain't fool enough to believe it."

Ky rides on Frank's shoulders, and I walk beside Pa toward the Phillipses' farm. Judging from the number of cars and buggies, neighbors have come from miles around. "Henry sure knows how to throw a party," Pa says.

I nod in agreement. I don't care much for Liza, but her dad is a nice man. "I bet Henry is not too happy losin' both Earl and J.T.," Pa says. "Both of 'em are hard workers."

"It's not like they're gone for good," I snap. "Winston is not that far!"

Pa raises his eyebrows at me. "Missy, you'd better remember who you're talkin' to." He moseys over to Mr. Phillips and slaps him on the back. "Need some help?" he asks.

Mr. Phillips points to the fire, where a cast-iron pot hangs from a trestle. "Stick around," he says. "I'll need an expert taster in a few minutes."

Pa grins. "Henry, I'm just the man to help you."

Leaving the menfolk, I follow Frank to the overhang attached to the tobacco barn. Underneath it, Liza's mama is fussing over the dessert table. "Hello, Jessie. Did you bake something?"

"No, ma'am. I brought a jar of apple butter and a jar of blackberry jam." I reach into the cloth bag slung over my shoulder and pull them out.

Standing near the overhang, J.T. and Earl hold court over the pretty girls from nearby farms. "Looks like you got here just in time," Frank whispers. "Liza has her arm linked with J.T.'s."

I take a deep breath and force a smile. "Yes, it does. It looks like I got here just in time to watch J.T. act like a horse's butt." I hold out my arms for Ky. "I'll take him over to where the toddlers are playing."

"Good idea," Frank says. "Ky would enjoy that." He swings Ky over his head and plops him into my arms. I make my way over to Sophie and let Ky run free.

"Rose Lynn is growing into a beauty," I say. What I leave out is that she could be Violet's twin.

Sophie nods. "She's a good baby. Already sleeping through the night, too."

Vivi escapes from Maude and runs toward me with her arms outstretched. "Jessie," she yells, "play with me."

I lean down to talk with her. "I need the help of a big girl," I say. "Can you take care of Baby Ky?"

"Yep." Vivi smiles and reaches for his hand.

"She's just like Anna," I tell Sophie. "Loves to be in charge."

Sophie wipes drool off Rose Lynn's face. "I think she's getting a tooth," she says. "Speaking of Anna, I had a letter from her a couple of days ago."

"Me too," I say. "Her temperature is normal and she's gaining weight. The signs are more hopeful than we ever had with Carrie."

Mrs. Pilcher interrupts and elbows me in the ribs. "Would you look at that," she says. "Every widow and spinster in the community is after Frank."

"Don't be ridiculous," Sophie says sharply, but I see just what Mrs. Pilcher means. Frank is drawing a bigger crowd than a tent revival. And judging from the smile on his face, he's enjoying it.

"Chicken stew is ready!" Mr. Phillips yells. "Come and get it!"

I take a deep breath, inhaling the scents of wood smoke and buttery chicken, two of my favorite smells on earth.

While Cole gets stew for us, I hunker down with Ky and Vivi at the family table. I watch Liza push against J.T.'s chest with her hands. She tosses her hair and laughs. By the time Cole takes his place beside me, I'm itching to slap her and stomp back home.

Crumbling a biscuit into Ky's stew, I can't help but hear the women's talk of husbands and babies. "Labor is not so bad," Sophie says.

Pansy Pilcher laughs. "I guess it's better than bein' gored to death by a bull." I remember Carrie panting and moaning. Though I don't say so, I think I'd rather take my chances against the bull.

At the next table, J.T. and Earl brag about their new jobs. "The pay sure beats farmin'," Earl says.

Liza bats her eyelashes. "I'll be visiting often so you boys won't get lonely." I wipe food off Ky's chin. I shouldn't have let Frank talk me into coming.

When Ky's tummy is full, he nestles against my chest, settling in for a nap. I cover him with a shawl, trying to eavesdrop without looking too obvious.

Viney stands. "Earl, I'll be back in a few minutes." She walks over to me and lifts Ky from my arms. "I'll keep an eye on him," she says. "Get over there and say goodbye to J.T."

J.T. stands up when I do. He meets me halfway between our tables. "You look beautiful, Jessie."

His voice makes me feel tingly from my hair roots down to my toes. "I came to tell you goodbye," I say. "And to wish you luck with your new job."

J.T. stares into my eyes as if we're the only two people here. "Let me walk you home," he says.

I don't trust myself to be alone with him. I'm about to say no, but I catch the frown on Liza's face, see her straining to hear the conversation between us. "The fiddle playing is about to start," I say. "We could stay and dance."

J.T. shakes his head and gives me a smile that would melt butter. "I'd rather be alone with you," he says.

My heart beats faster and suddenly I don't give a rip that he's going to Winston. All I want is to be alone with him. "Let's find Frank," I say. "I'll leave Ky with him."

We've got no business in the fishing shack. I should have made J.T. walk me straight home. He lifts my hair and lets it slide through his fingers. "Don't ever cut it," he says huskily. He kisses my forehead, my closed eyelids, the tip of my nose, and finally my lips. "Promise you'll wait for me," he says.

His words fuel a blazing anger in my chest. I grab his face between my hands and look up at him. "I'm not going anywhere," I say fiercely. "You're the one leaving."

J.T. pushes away from me and sighs. "You don't know what it's like for a sharecroppin' family. I want to give you a better life than that."

"Just wait," I plead. "Frank will remarry. Anna will come back home, and then I'll go with you. Maybe I could finish school and still become a teacher."

J.T. turns his back on me and rakes his hands through his straw-colored hair. "I can't. I start work on Monday. If I go back on my word, Reynolds may never give me another chance."

My fingers play with the buttons on my shirtwaist. I could take it off and pull J.T. onto the floor. Let him touch me all the places that Carrie and Anna said were private. His strong sense of honor would kick in, and he'd stay with me. I know he would.

I unfasten the first button, and then the second. My fingers pause as J.T. leans his forehead against the wall. "I only let Liza hug me to make you jealous," he says.

At the mention of her name, my hand curls into a fist. Tricking J.T. is like something she would do. I won't stoop that low.

I slip across the cabin floor and hug him from behind. "I'm sorry," I say.

J.T. turns and pulls me into his arms. "What are you sorry for?"

"Never mind," I say. "Just walk me home."

J.T. nods and gives me a look so full of longing that it fills up my chest and forms a knot in my throat. "Life was easier when we were just fishin' buddies," he says.

23 | MOONING OVER J.T.

Patches nestles on the ground beside Ky. "Play right here," I tell them. "I've got to fill up the wash pots and cook up some stink soup." I bend down and scratch Patches behind his ears. My dog has turned traitor. I believe he loves Ky even more than he loves me.

I wind water from the well, bucket after bucket. When both pots are full, I light a fire underneath them in the stone furnace. Sophie says Ky will probably wear diapers for at least another year. That seems like an eternity.

"Jay, Jay, Jay, Jay," Ky yells. That's his name for me. I give the diapers a stir with the sassafras stick and trot over to check on him.

"Patches is not a horse, Ky." I lift him off the dog's back, plop him on the ground, and reach into my pocket. "Look what I found. Grandpa carved a rabbit for you."

Ky takes the rabbit and smiles.

Back at the rock furnace, I scrub the diapers on a washboard and give them a final rinse. J.T. has been gone for a month now, and I've thought about him at least a thousand times. My face feels flush just remembering what he smells like, how it feels to be alone with him. I wonder if Liza has paid him a visit yet.

On my way to the clothesline I check on Ky. I watch him dig in the dirt with Patches close by. I bend down and hug Ky to my chest. "Jay, Jay, Jay, Jay," he says.

I pin the diapers to the line, and a warm June breeze flaps them back and forth. Whispering my thoughts out loud, I beg J.T. to come back to me. I sigh and pat Anna's latest letter in my overalls pocket. She's lonely too, missing Cole and Vivi. I pick up the empty clothes-basket and turn around. I don't see Ky.

I race to the spot where I left him and pick up the rabbit and spoon. "Ky! Ky, where are you?"

I hurry past the garden to the barn. *Please God*, I pray, *don't let the mule kick him or the hogs attack him. Just keep him safe.*

"Carrie," I murmur under my breath, "please help me find Ky."
The creek! Surely he couldn't have wandered that far, but if he did...
I speed toward it, fighting my way through the woods. Branches slap
against me. I imagine Ky face down in the water. "No, no, no!" I beg.
But there's no sign of him.

I stop and tug on my braid. Think! Where would he have gone?
I hear a piercing scream. I listen closer, move away from the water,
and tear through the woods. I run toward the house, gasping for
breath.

Patches howls, "Aarrhh, aarrhh."

"Keep it up, boy! Keep it up." I race past the barn. Stumble
through the plowed garden. Fight my way through the diapers flap-
ping in the breeze. The screams! I think they're coming from the
back porch.

When he sees me, Ky shrieks, "Jay, Jay, Jay!"

Oh, my God! There's so much blood. "Ky, baby, what happened?"

"Jay, Jay, Jay!" he says, clutching me with his bloody hand.
I snatch him from the cure chair Pa made for Carrie. There's broken
glass all around. I hurry into the kitchen and grab a clean dish towel.
Ky howls when I press it against the jagged cut.

"Sssh. It's going to be okay. Really it is." I blink back my own
tears, then grab a handful of towels and pack them around Ky's
hand. "We're going to Vivi's house," I tell him. "Maude will know
just what to do."

Patches runs ahead of us, barking as loud as a whole pack of dogs.
I hurry behind with Ky clutched to my chest. "Don't worry, don't
worry," I whisper.

I stumble, pitch forward, and almost fall. By some miracle I
regain my balance and keep running. Maude bustles out to the front
porch. "What in Sam Hill is goin' on?" she yells.

"It's Ky," I call. "He cut himself." By the time I get to Anna's
kitchen, Maude has water heating, a jar of moonshine out of the
cabinet, and her sewing basket open.

"Lay him on the table," she says, "and I'll take a look." Maude
unties the handkerchief and moves the towels aside. She pours some
warm water on a cloth and cleans the wound, causing Ky to scream
and kick. "He needs stitches," she tells me. "One of us will have to
hold him while the other one sews up his hand."

"I'll hold him," I say.

Maude nods. "Stitchin' up cuts is one of my talents." She pours water from the kettle over her needle. "Thread it for me," she says. "My eyesight ain't what it once was."

With the needle threaded, I lay my chest across Ky's legs so that he can't move. Next I grab his right arm with my left hand, and his left arm with my right. Tears pour from Ky's eyes. He screams as the needle goes in. I clamp his arms like a vise. "Hurry," I beg Maude. "Please hurry." The needle goes in and out, in and out. With each thrust Ky shrieks, fighting against me.

"Keep a tight grip on him," Maude says. "I'm all done, but now I need to put some salve on his hand and bandage it up."

A few minutes later I dry Ky's tears and kiss his cheeks. "You are a brave boy," I say. He hugs my neck and then toddles off to play with Vivi. He smiles as if nothing bad ever happened.

"Be real careful with his bandage," Maude tells her.

I sink down into a kitchen chair and bury my face in my hands. Maude pours a healthy dose of moonshine into a cup. "Drink this," she says. "For medicinal purposes."

The liquor burns my throat on the way down. My eyes water and my cough sputters. Maude pounds my back. "Moonshine is an acquired taste," she says. "But I'm right partial to it." I mop my face with a handkerchief and feel her staring at me. "What happened to Ky?" she asks.

I tell her the truth, even admitting that it was my glass on the porch that Ky cut himself on. "Some nights after he goes to sleep, I sit outside by myself. Watch the moon and the stars. I love him," I whisper, "but sometimes I can hardly wait for him to go to sleep. I crave a few minutes of peace and quiet."

Maude nods. "A long time ago when my young'uns waz underfoot, I felt the same way. Ky had an accident, pure and simple."

I look down at the table. Accident or not, I've got to pay more attention. Quit mooning over J.T. Carrie's words come back to me. *I found out that you're not a little girl anymore but a strong young woman.* My sister was wrong. But I aim to make those words come true. "Maude," I say, "tell me how you got to be so good at everything."

"Gumption, Jessie. It takes gumption."

24 | PASS IT ON

Around here we call August the dog days of summer. Sophie and Tom rock in matching chairs on their front porch. He cradles Rose Lynn in the crook of his left arm. They look happy. I think this baby has finally laid Violet's ghost to rest.

"Hey, Jessie," Tom calls, "take a load off."

I plop down on the porch steps and mop my neck with a bandana. "Maude gave me the night off from washing dishes," I say. Since tobacco season started, Pa and Frank and I have been eating supper with Cole and Maude. That arrangement suits us all. Maude's cooking beats mine to pieces, and Cole needs the company.

"Would you like a drink of water?" Sophie asks.

I nod and follow her to the kitchen. "I have a favor to ask."

Sophie pours two glasses of water and sits down at the long pine table. She motions with her hand for me to sit across from her. "How can I help, Jessie?"

I take a swig of water, trying to find the right words. "I promised Ma that I'd finish my schooling, and since you used to be a teacher, I figured maybe you could help me."

Sophie beams. "Your ma hoped one of her daughters would become a teacher. After Anna and Carrie married young, she had her hopes pinned on you."

I nod. That's the dream Ma passed on to me, but now it seems selfish to even consider it. "Do you *really* think I'd make a good teacher?"

Sophie sips her water before answering. "Yes. Yes, I do. You're patient with Vivi and Ky, and you were always one of my best students."

My face heats up at her praise. Since I'm the youngest, my sisters have always seemed more capable. "What would I need to do?"

Sophie clasps her hands together. "I'll speak with Miss Wilson," she says. "I'll bet you could pass the eighth-grade examination already. And then I'll tutor you on the high school curriculum."

"High school?" Most people I know stopped at eighth grade.

Sophie pushes her chair back. "Stay right here. I've got something for you."

When she returns to the kitchen, she's carrying a stack of books: *Sanford's Common School Arithmetic*, *Maury's Manual of Geography*, *A History of the United States*, and *Page's Theory and Practice of Teaching*. "Open one," she says, "and read the inscription."

"It says *Fannie Speer*." That was my ma's name before she married Pa. Right underneath her name, there's more, in the same handwriting. I read it silently: *To Sophie Binkley. Good luck with your schooling. It is my pleasure to help you.* I can almost hear Ma say those words.

Sophie smiles. "When I wanted to be a teacher, your ma lent me her books. I offered to give them back, but Anna and Carrie told me to keep them."

I hug the books to my chest, feeling their connection to Ma. She quit school after Pa asked her to marry him. I push them toward Sophie. "Would you write my name in there?"

She nods. "Let me get the inkwell and a pen." When she passes the books back to me, I open the top one. *To Jessie Pearl Hennings*, her inscription reads. *Learning is meant to be shared. Pass it on.*

We grow quiet, and it feels as solemn as a baptism. Finally I break the somber mood. "Neither one of us has a lot of free time," I say. "When would we work?"

Sophie rubs her forehead, considering it. "What about after church on Sundays? Some people would be offended that I'm teaching on the Lord's Day, but education is God's work. He's already got more ignorant children than he needs."

I put the books down and squeeze Sophie's hands. "I'll work hard. I promise."

She looks directly into my eyes. "Dream big. I graduated from the Appalachian Training School for Teachers. You would love the Blue Ridge Mountains. I just know it!"

"The mountains?" I remember Anna's letters. She says the mountains are beautiful, especially when they're covered in mist. "A part of me yearns to go," I say, "but I can't leave Ky." Then I laugh. "J.T. would think I've gone crazy, traipsing off to the mountains. And so would Pa."

Sophie stares at me for a long time. She strokes her chin. "Jessie," she says, "for just a minute, quit worrying about J.T and your family. What do *you* need to be happy?"

"I'm not sure, Sophie. Nobody ever asked me that before."

The kerosene lamp casts shadows on the map spread across the kitchen table. I draw a star marking Watauga County, where the school for teachers is located. With my index finger I trace North Carolina's coastline. All that water and I've never even seen it.

"Jessie," Frank whispers. "What are you doin' up this time of night? You won't be worth a plug nickel tomorrow."

I shake my head to fight off sleepiness. "I'm keeping a promise to Ma."

25 | FOLK REMEDIES

"Read to 'em in the kitchen," Maude says. "So I can hear."

I pull Anna's rocker near the cook stove and settle in for story time. Ky nestles his chubby bottom against my left thigh, and Vivi squeezes herself into the rocker beside me.

"Once upon a time there were four little rabbits, and their names were..."

"Flopsy, Mopsy, Cotton-tail, and Peter," Vivi says. She almost knows the story by heart.

I read about Peter's mother telling him and his sisters not to enter Mr. McGregor's garden.

"He was a bad bunny," Vivi says.

Ky nods. "Bad bunny."

Both children suck in their breath as Mr. McGregor chases Peter. "Run, run, run!" Ky says.

When Peter escapes from the garden, Vivi and Ky clap.

"Another one," Vivi begs. And so I read *The Tale of Benjamin Bunny*.

"I enjoy them stories myself," Maude says. "Who'd you say wrote 'em?"

"Beatrix Potter."

"Never heard of her," Maude says. "I guess she ain't from around here."

While I help Maude finish supper, Cole lets himself in the back door. He ruffles Ky's hair, then crushes Vivi into a bear hug. "Did Frank and your pa head out early?"

I nod. "It was before daylight. I hope the tobacco brings a good price."

"Me too," Cole says. "Farmers with money in their pockets are good for business." He reaches over and sneaks a piece of fatback meat.

"I saw you," Maude says. "Give me a dad-burned minute to get it on the table."

Cole turns to me. "Jessie, you and Ky are welcome to stay here."
I stop for a minute and consider it. We've never been alone in the house overnight. "I don't think any spooks will get us," I say. "And besides, I'll get more studying done if I'm by myself."

Cole pats his shirt pocket. He always carries Anna's latest letter there. "She's proud of you," he says. "Her doctor says she's gettin' better every day."

I tug on my braid. "Do you think she'll be home in time for Christmas?"

Cole looks down at his big feet. "No," he says. "Not this year."

Maude flips a pone of cornbread onto a plate and dishes up black-eyed peas and potatoes. "Enough sad talk," she says. "It'll ruin your digestion."

Tonight the algebra problems muddle my brain. "Come on, Jessie," I tell myself. "Just assign an X to the unknown variable and solve the darn thing."

But it's no use. All I can think about is Ky. I'm the one he runs to when he skins his knees. The one he expects to feed him and clean his bottom. I'll never leave here as long as he needs me.

I close the book and push away from the table. I hear a grunt followed by a bark. The sound sends shivers up my spine. Then another grunt and a bark. I pick up the lamp and creep down the hall. My God! The sound is coming from Ky's room!

I move faster now, and shine the light on Ky's tear-stained face. With each breath in, he grunts. It's followed by a hoarse, barking cough. I put the lamp down, snatch him from the crib, and cradle him in my arms.

"Sssh. It's okay," I whisper. "Aunt Jessie is here." I fight to keep my voice even, not to let him see my panic. I've never heard such sounds from a human being.

I pace around his room, rubbing his back, and whispering that everything will be okay. I remember Doc saying that about half the babies born to mothers with TB get sick too. "Please God," I beg, "don't take him away from me. I'd rather die myself." Ky's cough worsens. The grunts sound deeper, the barking more hoarse.

I consider taking him to Maude. But it's pitch black outside, and I don't think I can manage carrying a sick baby plus a lantern.

Frank's Model T sits in the shed. Curse me for a fool: I've never driven it.

Ky fights to breathe, and it reminds me of Carrie. Being outside often helped her. I wrap Ky in a blanket and hurry to the front porch. The crisp October air chills me but seems to ease his coughs a bit.

I pace back and forth on the porch. Back and forth. I need Maude or my sisters. Somebody full of wisdom to tell me what to do. Anna's voice plays inside my head like a phonograph. *Silly girl, you have Ma's home remedies.*

I tear through the house, clutching Ky in my arms. I place him on my bed and hurry to the bureau. Reaching inside the bottom drawer, I shove aside the clean pair of overalls and pull out the book Anna left for me. I thumb through the pages to the home remedies: hives, headache, sore mouth, sick stomach, heartburn. Where's the one I need? Hallelujah, here it is! *For a barking cough, mix a spoonful of sugar with a spoonful of beaten alum.*

Maude used alum to can the pickles. Please God, let there be some left. I hurry with Ky to the kitchen and place him in his high chair. I find alum in the canning closet, grind it with a pestle, and mix it with sugar. I coax the concoction into Ky's mouth a little at a time. "Come on, sweetie, come on, this will make it all better."

Ky's coughs finally ease, and he holds out his arms toward me. I take him from his high chair, clutching him to my chest. "Jay, Jay, Jay," he says.

I carry him to my bed, afraid to let him out of my sight, and reach for Ma's journal again. This time I read it slowly, hoping to find what caused the terrible barking. A feeling of relief shoots through me when I get to the right part. I close my eyes and offer up a prayer. "We haven't been on speaking terms since Carrie died, but thank you for helping me. I am mighty grateful that Ky doesn't have tuberculosis."

I hug the book to my chest. Croup is nothing serious, but my nerves are about shot. If Maude were here, I'd ask her for another cup of moonshine.

26 | THE MODEL T AND ME

I wait until Frank is in a good mood, his stomach full of beans and potatoes. "November is a slow time of year," I say.

Frank nods. "Yep. Now that the crops are in, all that's left is to cut plenty of wood. Time to hunker down for the winter."

I take a seat beside him on the settee. "I've been thinking. Now that you've got some free time, you could teach me to drive."

Frank's eyes bug out of his head. "Women and cars don't mix," he says. "Priscilla Phillips backed through the henhouse. Henry has put his foot down. No women drivers in his family."

"That's just ignorant," I say, and cross my arms. "What if Ky had really needed a doctor while you were at the tobacco sale? What if he had died because I couldn't get help?"

Frank winces at such plain talk. "Don't ever say that again," he says. "If Ky had died, I'd hang myself from the nearest tree."

I keep staring at him. I don't plan to back down.

After what seems like an eternity, he walks over to the front door. "Come on. I ain't got all day."

Frank talks about his Model T as if it's a woman. "First make sure she's got gasoline," he says. He raises the seat cushion and shows me the gas tank underneath. He checks the fuel level with a dipstick. He makes sure the radiator is filled with water and that there's enough oil in the crankcase.

I climb over the low door, glad for my overalls. Frank gets in the passenger side. "See the tall lever stickin' up from the floor? It controls the parkin' brake," he says. "Always set it first thing."

"Why?" I ask.

"If you were to crank her without the brake on, she could move forward and mow you down."

I nod. "I won't be forgetting that one anytime soon."

He points to another lever on the left, beneath the steering column. "That one retards the spark," he says. "Move it up." And so I do.

He takes hold of my right hand and guides it to the lever on the right side of the steering column. "The throttle gives her gasoline," he says. "Pull it down a few notches."

"Okay, throttle down."

"Now turn the switch, and put it in the battery position." The T buzzes like a bee.

"This is the quietest you've ever been," Frank teases. "If I'd a knowed it would shut you up, I'd a taught you to drive long ago."

"Quit teasing me so that I can concentrate. I plan to be a really good driver."

We climb out and stand in front of the car. "Pull the choke wire," Frank says. "See it pokin' out down here? Now you're ready to crank!"

I stare at the crank. Lots of folks have broken their arms cranking a Model T.

"The secret," Frank says, "is not to wrap your thumb around the handle." He shows me how to hold it.

Getting up my nerve, I give it a mighty tug, but the T doesn't start. I grab the crank again and pull harder and faster.

The motor roars to life, but my heartbeat sounds louder. "I cranked it!" I yell. "I cranked that sucker!"

"Not bad for a girl," Frank says. "Now climb inside and advance the spark." He listens to the engine. "A little more, little more. There you go. Now flip the switch from battery to magneto."

I rev her up a little and release the parking brake. "Nice and slow," Frank says. "Use your left foot and push down on the gear pedal."

I give her some gas with my right fingers, and we lurch onto the dirt road. My hands grip the steering wheel in a chokehold. I stare straight ahead. And I'm praying. Praying we don't meet any cars. Or wagons either.

"Take your foot off the pedal," Frank yells. "This Tin Lizzie is ready for high gear!"

I get her up to fifteen miles an hour. We sail by the Phillipses' farm with no problem whatsoever. "I think I'm pretty good at this," I say. But then a chicken crosses the road. I swerve to avoid it but slam into it anyhow. Feathers fly toward heaven. "Dad-burn it! I've killed a chicken!"

Frank chuckles. "I guess Henry ain't got around to rebuildin' the henhouse," he says. "Keep goin'."

I drive by the Pilcher farm and by Viney's house. I sure wish she were outside to see me.

"Go on to Meyers's store," Frank says. "We'll buy some penny candy."

I grin at him. "That sounds good, but you need to tell me again how to stop this contraption."

Frank points and talks me through the steps. We coast to a stop beside a Model T with gleaming black paint. "Belongs to Henry Phillips," he says. "Even has one of those new electric starters."

I leave him to admire Mr. Phillips's Model T and head inside. "Afternoon, Mr. Meyers."

"Nice to see you, Jessie. Need any help?"

"Nah, just looking." I peer into the candy case at the peppermints and lemon drops.

Liza Phillips saunters up beside me. "I saw you driving that old Tin Lizzie. Pa gave ours to Earl and now we have a newer model. It doesn't even have to be hand-cranked."

I smile at her all sweet-like. "That must be nice," I say. "But of course it doesn't really matter, since your pa won't let you drive it."

Liza's face scrunches into an ugly frown. "You are mean as the devil, Jessie Hennings. I guess that's why J.T. hasn't been back for a visit."

I keep the smile pasted to my face. "Mr. Meyers, I'll take some peppermints." I turn to Liza. "You don't know squat about me and J.T. He told my pa he wants to marry me when I turn eighteen."

Liza laughs. "Earl has driven home to see Viney, but J.T. can't be bothered with you. I guess things changed once he got to Winston."

I pay Mr. Meyers and take my bag of peppermints. "Liza, don't you worry your empty head about me. I've applied to the Appalachian Training School for Teachers. If J.T. changes his mind, I'm smart enough to have a backup plan."

Liza's eyes narrow. "I don't believe you," she says, "and how in the world would you pay for it?"

I flounce across the store and turn around at the door. "Watch and see. I've got a bright future ahead of me."

Sophie is sweeping leaves off her front porch when Frank and I pull into the driveway. She drops the broom and rushes down the steps.

"I bet Tom a butter churning that you'd give in and teach Jessie to drive!"

Frank laughs. "Jessie's a pest, and I got tired of arguin' with her."

I climb out of the car. "Frank, I appreciate the lesson. I'll walk home after I visit with Sophie."

We watch him back the car down the driveway, before turning toward the house. "What's wrong?" Sophie asks. "Your face looks like a thundercloud."

I wait until we're in the kitchen before answering. "It's that empty-headed Liza Phillips. We had a terrible argument about J.T. at Frank Meyers's store. I'm ready to fill out the application for teachers' school."

Sophie rises from her seat. "Let's have a cup of tea," she says. She puts water in the kettle and sets out cups and saucers. "Jessie, I do think you should apply, but not when you're feeling hurt and angry."

I tug on my braid. "I should have slapped Liza, and then I'd feel better. Why do you think I should apply?"

Sophie pours tea through the strainer and pushes a plate of cookies toward me. "Because you're different from your sisters. Anna is a doer, and Carrie was a dreamer. But you? You are an adventurer."

I smile because she has my sisters pegged. "What exactly makes me different?"

"Well, you'd rather hunt and fish than do housework. You love the threshing machine and poring over maps. Do you really feel ready to settle down?"

I bite into a cookie, considering all she's said. "I want to go away to school, but I don't want to leave Ky...or lose J.T."

Sophie sips her tea. "Jessie, do you believe J.T. loves you?"

I nod. "I think so, but why hasn't he been home? Or even written to me?"

Sophie reaches out and touches my hand. "I can't explain why you haven't heard from him. But he's off chasing his dreams. Don't you deserve the same chance?"

I stand up and start pacing. "You know it's different for a woman. I'm expected to be the one to accommodate him."

Rose Lynn shrieks, and Sophie rises from her chair. "Don't leave," she says. "I'll be right back."

I'm still pacing when Sophie carries Rose Lynn to the kitchen.

"Jessie, there's no reason to make a decision today. Serious choices deserve long consideration."

Sophie's right, but I don't want to wait forever on a boy who may never come back to me.

27 | MOONSHINE

I place Ky on the trundle bed and pull up the quilt. "Sweet dreams, pumpkin." I watch him sleep and admit the truth: I was mad when I mailed the application. As long as Ky needs me, I'll be right here. I bend over and place a kiss on his cheek.

When I'm sure he's settled for the night, I join Pa and Frank in the parlor. "You two are awfully quiet," I say.

Pa looks up from his whittling. "Louder, girl, I can't hear you." He holds up the figure he's carving for Ky. "Can you guess who this is?"

I laugh at the stubborn expression and straw hat. There's no doubt which animal Pa is copying. "It's Patience! Ky loves that ornery mule."

Pa keeps whittling and Frank dozes on the settee. He jerks awake at a screeching, tearing noise. "What the devil is that?" he asks. The sounds get louder. Grinding, popping, exploding! We're rooted to our seats, stunned by the terrible racket. But a woman's screams send us scrambling for the door.

Frank jerks it open. "Grab the lantern," he yells. "There's been an accident."

Pa and Frank rush outside, and I'm left to light the lantern. Parts of a Model T are scattered on the road, in the ditch, and in the woods across from our house. The strong stench of corn liquor mixes with the night air.

Frank is kneeling beside the ditch. "Hezekiah, there's a man down here!" he yells.

Pa hurries over and peers into the ditch too. "Can you tell if he's alive?"

"Just help me climb out," a deep voice grumbles. "I'm more drunk than hurt." Pa and Frank both reach out a hand and hoist the man onto level ground.

It's Rafe Allman. His eyes are bloodshot and he looks around with a panicked expression. "Where's Liza? I was givin' her a drivin' lesson."

Frank shakes his head. "Teachin' her at night and when you're full of moonshine? Her pa will see to it that you're tarred and feathered."

I step over twisted metal, engine parts, and a busted tire. "Liza," I yell. "Liza, where are you?"

"She's over here," Pa calls. Liza's eyes are closed, and she's bleeding from a gash near her hairline. Her skirt is bunched up around her thighs.

"I might a missed her," Pa says, "if not for those white bloomers shinin' in the dark. Maybe you should make her decent, and I'll carry her to the house."

I rip Liza's petticoat and tie a strip of it around her forehead. Then I pull her skirt down and Pa lifts her into his arms.

I shine the lantern so that he won't trip over all the scattered parts. "How is she?" Frank asks. Rafe doesn't speak, just hangs his head.

"Unconscious," Pa says. "No way to tell how bad her injuries are. I'd say you should go for Doc, and I'll fetch Henry and Priscilla."

I hold the front door open for Pa. "Put her in my room," I say. I turn down the quilt, and he places Liza on my bed. The petticoat strip is already soaked with blood.

"Stay with her," Pa says, "and I'll boil some water."

Liza looks pale, her skin white as milk. "Wake up," I beg. "Don't you dare die in my bed. I'm sure you'd haunt me for all eternity." I touch her clammy hand and rub it between my own, trying to warm it up.

Pa brings in a basin of water. "You'd best stitch that cut," he says. "She's losing too much blood."

"But I've never stitched a cut before. I've only watched Maude."

His dark eyes stare into mine. "I got no doubt you'll do a fine job."

I go for Ma's sewing basket and thread the needle. I untie the petticoat strip and clean the wound.

Pa reaches out and steadies my hand. "I'll hold on to Liza, in case she wakes up."

He pins her body to the mattress, and I push the needle in and out, making fifteen tiny, perfect stitches. Liza doesn't stir.

"I'll ride over to the Phillipses' farm now," Pa says. "Be back in a few minutes."

I pull the quilt up to Liza's chin. Sneaking around with a moonshiner. Sometimes she doesn't have the brains that God gave a stump.

Her eyelids flutter and she moans. "What happened?" Her hand reaches up and brushes the bandage around her head. "Hurts."

"It's Jessie," I say. "You were in a car crash with Rafe Allman."

Liza rubs her eyes and peers up at me. "This is all your fault. Oh, my head! Why do you make me act so stupid?"

I cross my arms. "Explain it to me," I say. "I'm pretty simple-minded. How is it my fault you were out with Rafe Allman?"

"Because you push me to do crazy things," Liza says. "After we had that argument, I was determined to learn how to drive. When my pa said no, I went looking for Rafe. He told me to slip out as soon as it was dark. He had a load of moonshine to deliver, but he'd teach me to drive after he dropped it off."

I grin at Liza. "From the looks of things, he's not a very good teacher."

She scowls. "Rafe's a drunken oaf! We delivered the shine, but he kept a pint to drink on the way home. He was driving too fast and pawing at me. When I punched him in the nose, he lost control of the car."

I slap my thigh and laugh. "I didn't know you could land a punch."

"I learned from watching Earl and J.T.," she says, "but I never had the nerve to hit anybody before tonight."

While Doc examines Liza, I make a pot of coffee. Frank comes in and sits down at the table. "Your pa is in the parlor with Priscilla and Henry. I'd advise Rafe to take off for the hills. Henry is hoppin' mad."

"I sure hope Mr. Phillips and Rafe won't meet up tonight," I say. "We've had enough excitement." While I'm waiting for the coffee to percolate, I tell Frank how Liza socked Rafe in the nose. "I didn't know she had it in her!"

Frank grins. "Sounds like Rafe had it comin'. Liza's a right pretty girl...and feisty too."

Frank looks pleased as punch. "Henry Phillips is payin' me a quarter an hour to teach Liza to drive. He's buyin' the gas and lettin' me use his new car too."

Pa chuckles. "Gettin' paid to ride around with a pretty girl—it's a hard job, but I guess somebody's got to do it."

I stack the supper dishes and move them to the sink. Frank is taking Liza out almost every afternoon. If you ask me, nothing good can come from it. Ky bangs on his high chair. "Hand him a cookie," I say.

Frank drops the cookie and it crumbles on the floor. When he reaches for another one, I notice that his hands are shaking. Out of nowhere, he says, "I'll always love Carrie."

Pa takes a sip of his coffee. "I 'spect you will. Same as I'll always love Jessie's mama."

Frank blushes and taps his foot. "You might as well spill the beans," I say. "What's bothering you?"

"Thanksgiving," he blurts out. "I'd like to invite Liza for Thanksgiving."

Pa meets Frank's gaze and nods. "You were a fine husband to Carrie," he says. "Liza is welcome in my house."

I turn toward the sink and scrub the plates hard enough to rub off all the shine.

"Jessie," Frank says. "What do you think? Your opinion matters to me."

I drop the soapy cloth in the sink. "Why her?" I ask. "She's been my enemy ever since we started school."

Frank looks like I just slapped him. "You're both grown up now. I was hopin' you'd put all that foolishness behind you."

I shrug. "Ten years of fighting is hard to forget."

I can feel Frank staring at my back. "I want to bring her here," he says. "But I won't ruin your Thanksgiving. I'll take Ky and we'll eat with Liza's family."

I grip the plate hard, wishing I could throw it at his fool head. "I have spent the last year taking care of Ky, but you'll steal him away from me? For Liza Phillips?"

"Jessie," Pa says. "Stop it. Don't say anything you'll regret."

I look up at the ceiling, determined not to cry. Chairs scrape against the floor as Frank and Pa push back from the table. The high chair squeaks when Frank lifts Ky out. Their footsteps echo down the hall.

Finally alone, I let the tears fall. Sometimes it seems there is no justice in this world. Not one bit.

Though Anna's house is larger, everybody prefers holidays here. Maybe it's because of tradition, or memories of Ma.

"We've got a lot to be thankful for," Sophie says. "I really believe Anna will be coming home soon."

Maude opens the oven door and bastes the turkey. "Needs about another hour," she says.

Sophie adds a little more salt to the potatoes. "Jessie, why don't you run and change into a dress?"

I shrug. "What's the point?"

I hear doors slam and Cole's booming voice. "Welcome, Liza. What's underneath that cloth?"

I can't make out her answer, but I'm sure it's baked to perfection. Liza sashays into the kitchen. "It's nice to see all of you. I brought a pecan pie."

"That sounds delicious," Sophie says. "Maude, do you remember Liza? She was here after Carrie's funeral."

Maude looks Liza over head to toe. "Yep, I remember her. You can put the pecan pie on the table."

Liza puts the pie down and twists her hands as if she's nervous. "Hello, Jessie."

"Hey, Liza."

Her right hand sweeps her honey-colored hair off her forehead. "Thank you for stitching me up. Doc says he couldn't have done a better job himself."

Maude elbows her way across the kitchen. "Let me see." She rubs her index finger across the faint scar. "I taught Jessie how to stitch up a wound. She's like me. Can do anything she sets her mind to."

I stare at Liza. She's wearing a wool serge dress with white collar and cuffs. The rich brown color shows off her blond hair and makes her eyes look dark as chocolate. "I'd like to help," she tells Maude. "Do you have a job for me?"

Maude hands her a bowl of melted butter and a brush. "You can baste the turkey's butt," she says.

There's barely room to squeeze around the table. Ky and Rose Lynn are both in high chairs, and Vivi climbs into my lap. "Get down from there," Cole booms. "Your aunt Jessie won't be able to eat her dinner."

I shake my head. "She's fine. Vivi can sit with me." Actually I don't have much appetite, and I'm glad to hide behind her.

Pa asks everybody to hold hands.

"Dear Lord," he prays. "Last year about this time, we weren't sure how to get through the comin' year without Carrie. I want to thank you for seein' us through. Thank you for my new granddaughter, Rose Lynn. And for Maude and Jessie, who stepped in and held us together. And I'm askin' a special blessin' on my daughter, Anna. We'd sure be grateful if she could come home soon. Amen."

After a chorus of Amens, Maude starts passing side dishes around the table. "Sweet potatoes, mashed, or a little of both?" she asks.

Sophie smiles at me. "I'll fill your plate. You've got your hands full with Vivi."

"Liza," Cole booms, "how are the drivin' lessons comin' along? I told Frank he should incorporate. Call his company Logan's School for Female Drivers."

Liza lowers her eyes and smiles a secret sort of smile. "I wouldn't want to share my teacher," she says. "He's very talented."

I peek around Vivi and focus on Frank. He's gazing at Liza the way he used to look at Carrie. I'd bet my bottom dollar he's teaching her more than how to drive.

Sophie reaches out and touches my arm. "Jessie," she whispers, "don't let Liza bother you. Try to eat your dinner."

"Don't worry. I'm fine."

Liza reaches out with a napkin and wipes Ky's face. He gives her a big, toothy smile. I want to slap her hand away, tell her never to touch my baby again.

Finally even Cole has had his fill. "I couldn't eat another bite if you paid me," he says.

"My compliments to the cooks," Frank adds.

Maude stands and waves her hand like a fly flap. "Men to the parlor and take the children with you."

While Liza and Sophie clear the table, I head outside and wind two buckets of water from the well. Maude looks up when I bring them into the kitchen. "I've got plenty of help," she says. "Why don't you whistle for that fool dog of yours? Take a walk and clear your head."

I don't usually hug Maude, but now I wrap my arms around her ample middle.

"Ah, go on with you," she says. "Be back in time for pumpkin pie and coffee."

Patches comes running and we head toward the fishing shack. My brogans crunch against the frozen ground, and I ache for J.T. Ache to see his smile, feel his hair tangled in my fingers, his arms holding me tight.

I let myself in the cabin and pull up a chair. I close my eyes, reliving every time I was here with him.

I can see the future barreling toward me like a runaway train. Liza living in my house and raising Ky. Stop it, I tell myself. Face the truth. Frank is finally happy. And Carrie wanted him to remarry. She only asked me to step in until Frank found a wife. Her letter haunts me. *Choose your second wife wisely.* My gut tells me Liza is not the right choice. *Be sure she can love our son with all her heart.* Liza has always been stuck on herself. I don't believe she can put Ky first, but the only way to find out is to ask her.

29 | THE TRUTH ABOUT J.T.

When I push the cabin door open, Liza stumbles in. "What are you doing here?" I ask. "I was just on my way back to the house to find you."

Liza burrows into her fur-trimmed coat. "I have to talk to you."

I close the door against the cold wind and shove my reddened fingers into my pockets. "Go ahead. I'm listening."

Liza walks over to the window and leans her forehead against the pane. "You and I are like the Hatfields and McCoys," she says. "I don't even remember why we started feuding."

I shrug. "*Why* isn't really important. What I remember is your sharp tongue. Always trying to make me feel poor and plain."

Liza turns from the window. "I was jealous. From the time I was a little girl, I worshipped J.T. But he never showed one ounce of interest in me. I couldn't figure it out. Why would he prefer you over me?" She sweeps her hand toward my clothes. "You could never be bothered to put on a dress or even comb your hair."

I shake my head. "There's no logical way to explain it. J.T. and I just belong together."

Liza's expression gets all dreamy. "That's how I feel about Frank. Like we belong together. J.T. was just a schoolgirl's crush."

I search Liza's face, looking for any trace of the hateful girl I've always known. "What about Ky?" I ask. "Frank comes with a son."

Liza meets my gaze and doesn't look away. "He's the spitting image of Frank," she says. "How could I help but love him?"

I close my eyes, looking deep inside for the strength to forgive her, but there's no way. "I'll try and tolerate you," I say, "as long as you're good to Ky."

Liza wraps her arms around her body and shivers. "Jessie, I have one more sin to confess, and it's a big one."

A feeling of dread takes root in my chest.

"Try to remember that I've changed," Liza says. "I'm really

sorry. I'd take it back if I could." She reaches into her coat pocket and pulls out a packet of letters. She thrusts them toward me. My name is on the envelope on top, scrawled in J.T.'s handwriting.

I snatch the letters from her hand. "Where did you get these?"

"I've been clerking in the post office."

"You *stole* them?" Fast as greased lightning, I slap her hateful face. The sound echoes like a gunshot and Liza screams.

Her fingers rub the handprint that I left across her cheek. "Liza!" Frank yells, and pushes his way inside without knocking. "Sweetheart, are you all right?"

Frank hurries to Liza and wraps her in his arms. "Jessie, what in the hell is wrong with you?"

Angry tears shimmer in my eyes. I wave the packet of letters. "Do you see these? Liza has been stealing my letters from J.T."

Frank rests his chin on top of Liza's head and she sobs against his chest. "I'm sure there's some kind of a mixup," he says.

"Save me from pig-headed fools," I say. "Just because she has the face of an angel doesn't mean she has the heart of one. She stole the letters on purpose. Just ask her."

Liza raises her tear-stained face. "I did steal them on purpose," she sobs. "But I'm so...so...sorry."

I walk over to the door and turn the knob. "Frank, I can't stop you from seeing her, but you need to remember Carrie's letter. Think long and hard about the kind of mother Ky needs. If you've got a brain left in your head, you'll take Liza home and never look back!"

Snuggled in the hayloft with Patches, I read J.T.'s letters. In May he wrote, *Factory work is easy compared to farming. But it's boring too.* In June he tells me, *The factory is stifling hot, and I miss working outside.* July's letter begs me to write. *I know you're stubborn, but it would mean the world to me to hear from you.*

I hurry through the letters for August, September, and October. Finally I come to the last one. *A girl who works in payroll asked me to supper. She cooked a nice meal, but I feel guilty for going. It's hard to hang on when you won't answer my letters. I still love you, Jessie, but I need to know whether you feel the same way.*

I start to scream, using the bale of hay as a punching bag. I'd like to kick Liza's sorry butt all around this farm.

"Jessie," Frank yells, "get down here and discuss this like an adult."

105

I pitch the bale of hay from the loft, barely missing his head. "Get that lying piece of trash off our land!" I shriek.

"I already took her home," Frank shouts, "and told her I wouldn't see her anymore. I hope you're satisfied!"

30 | AN UNEXPECTED PROPOSAL

"Jessie," Pa says, "the Christmas Eve service starts in a couple of hours. You'd best get dressed."

I open the oven door and pull out a tray of sugar cookies. "I'm not going, Pa."

He raises his eyebrows and gives me a stern look.

"Cookies! Cookies!" Ky yells, racing into the kitchen.

Pa catches him just before he crashes into the oven door. "Stop it, boy! You'll get burned!"

Frank follows close behind. "Sorry, he got away from me. Jessie, I heard what you said. Are you stayin' home because of Liza?"

I know that Frank hasn't seen her since Thanksgiving, but he's looked as droopy as an old hound dog ever since.

"I'm tired of all this foolishness," Pa says. "Now Jessie, get in there and put on a dress."

I sigh and figure the truth is the quickest way out. "I don't have a dress. I've grown a couple of inches taller and filled out some. Nothing fits me anymore."

Frank walks over and stands beside me. My head reaches the top of his shoulders. "You're exactly Carrie's height," he says. "And I'd be willin' to bet you're the size she was before she took sick."

He grabs my hand and pulls me into his bedroom. "Her things are in the closet. She'd want you to have them."

I throw my arms around Frank's waist and hug him. "I'm sorry. I've hated fighting with you."

He kisses the top of my head. "I'll put Ky down for a quick nap. Now take those clothes and get dressed."

Carrie's navy velveteen dress is a perfect fit. I check the mirror, stunned by how much I look like her. I comb out my hair and think of J.T. He's had time to get my letter. I pray he'll be home for Christmas.

Frank whistles when I walk into the parlor. "You look beautiful," he says. "Just like Carrie."

I spin around so that Pa and Frank can admire the dress. I stop in mid-twirl and race for Ky's room. "What's that noise?" Frank yells.

Gathering Ky against my chest, I whisper, "Sssh, sweet boy. Sssh. Aunt Jessie will fix it."

Frank is as pale as a bedsheet. "What's wrong? He sounds awful!"

"Croup. Take him outside while I mix up sugar and alum."

With shaking hands I beat the alum and add sugar. Pa watches me from the kitchen doorway. "Is there anything I can do to help?"

I stir the mixture together. "Nope, I've got it under control. But we won't be going to church."

Pa nods. "Guess I'll change out of my Sunday best. Holler if you need me."

I hurry outside and find Frank cradling Ky on the porch swing. His cough sounds like a dog's bark. Ky reaches out his arms, wanting me to comfort him. "I'll cuddle in just a minute. First you have to take your medicine."

When Ky's better, Frank hands him to me and sets the swing rocking with his foot. My hugs and the gentle motion put Ky to sleep within minutes.

Frank takes a deep breath. "You smell like her. Like Carrie. Did you know that?"

I shake my head. "No," I whisper. "I didn't know."

Frank reaches out and touches my hair. "So soft. Just like hers." He looks at me with such longing, but he's seeing a ghost.

A shudder passes through his body. "Missin' her is like bein' sick with a fever that never lets up."

I take his hand. "I'm sorry, Frank. I miss her too."

His voice breaks and he's struggling not to cry. "I've been watchin' you with Ky. You're a good mother, Jessie. The best."

His words make all of the hard times seem worthwhile. "You too," I say. "You're a wonderful father."

Frank leans forward and brushes his lips across mine. "Do you think we could learn to love each other, Jessie? Get married and raise Ky together? Maybe give him brothers and sisters someday?"

He deepens the kiss, and I'm too shocked to resist.

Ky stirs against me in his sleep, and I gently push Frank away. "I love you, and I always will...but it's the same kind of love I feel for Tom."

He leans back against the porch swing and puts his hands over his eyes. "I'm sorry, Jessie. I don't know what came over me. For a minute it seemed like you were Carrie."

We keep rocking in the cold night air. What happened shows me how deep his sorrow is, how much he needs a wife.

"Frank," I ask, "do you love Liza?"

He takes his time answering. "It's too soon for that. But she made me feel good again." He sighs. "I'm so tired of bein' miserable."

I lean over and kiss his cheek. "It's still early. Go see her."

Frank shakes his head. "Jessie Pearl, I'll never understand you. Liza did a terrible thing. Why are you changin' your mind?"

"Because I've had a month to cool off, and I think maybe she has grown up. The old Liza would have burned those letters. She would never have owned up to making a mistake."

"Is that the only reason?"

I shake my head. "No, you took my side against Liza. You even put how I was feeling over your own happiness. Your loyalty means a lot to me."

Frank stands and helps me to my feet. "Don't worry," he says, "I'll take it slow. I owe it to Carrie to find a good mother for Ky."

"Read her letter again. It'll keep you from making a mistake."

He holds the door for me to take Ky inside. "Merry Christmas, Jessie. I hope you get whatever it is you're wishin' for."

Wood curls fall from Pa's whittling knife onto the parlor floor. "Thought I'd carve Peter Rabbit for Ky's stocking. How's he doin'?"

"Much better," I say. "Would you like some hot chocolate and sugar cookies?"

Pa looks up from the block of wood. "Sit with me a minute, Jessie. I'm like that Dickens fellow, haunted by the Ghost of Christmas Past."

I throw a log into the woodstove and pull my chair closer. "Which Christmas is haunting you, Pa?"

More wood shavings roll off his knife. "The last one I spent with your ma. Fannie had baked a spice cake and the house smelled all sweet-like. We hadn't been scarred by death yet. Had everything in the world that really mattered, but didn't appreciate it near enough."

My rocker creaks against the wood floor, and I close my eyes, wishing for Ma, Carrie, and J.T.

"That's a dreamy look on your face," Pa teases. "Must be thinkin' of your sweetheart."

"I'm thinking of last Christmas, when J.T. gave me my treasure box."

A roaring engine snaps me back to the present, and I hurry to the door. Cole's car pulls into the driveway, with Tom's right behind it.

"Everything all right?" Cole yells. "We missed you at church." As he helps Maude from the car, Vivi comes running.

"Jessie, Jessie, see my new dress!"

"It's beautiful, Vivi. I have a ribbon for your hair that will just match it." I hold the door open as Cole, Maude, Sophie, and Tom all tramp inside. "Is Rose Lynn asleep?" I whisper.

"Slept through the whole service," Tom says.

"You can put her in the cradle in my room."

Pa smiles as the family crowds into the parlor. He rises and puts his arm around my shoulders. "Now's the perfect time for cookies and hot chocolate," he says.

Maude follows me to the kitchen, and I rummage in the cabinet for the Hershey's cocoa. "Have you heard from your young man?" she asks.

I busy myself mixing the cocoa, sugar, and salt. "Not a word. I'm afraid he's got another girl."

Maude fills two plates with sugar cookies. "How much do you love this boy?" she asks.

Her question makes me all teary-eyed. "A lot," I whisper. "Liza stole his letters to me. I guess she finally came between us."

Maude nods. "I heard the whole story from Frank, and then I cornered Liza in the post office. Had myself a come-to-Jesus talk with her."

I laugh, adding water to the cocoa mixture. A lecture from Maude is bound to be a scary thing. I put the pan on the stove to heat. "What's your opinion of Liza?"

Maude takes a seat at the table. "She wanted to hurt you, and it came back to bite her in the backside. I do think she regrets it, and I'd bet the farm she loves Frank."

I stir the cocoa as it comes to a boil. "Yes, I think you're right. Since she makes Frank happy, I need to learn to tolerate her."

Our conversation is interrupted by the sound of tires on gravel. "Maude," I yell, "do you hear that? Everybody else is here. It's got to be J.T.!"

She gives me a big smile. "Well, don't just stand there."

I smooth my hair and take off running. When I jerk the door open and see who it is, I have to hide my disappointment. "Come on in. You're just in time for hot chocolate."

Liza takes Frank's hand and gives me a nervous smile. "Merry Christmas, Jessie."

Pa lifts Ky from his high chair. "Now that his belly is full of pancakes, I'll take him with me to check the rabbit traps."

I pour myself another cup of coffee before answering. "Good idea," I say. "Get his heavy coat and mittens."

Frank pushes his chair back. "I'll help Jessie with the dishes...on account of it's Christmas."

I raise my eyebrows at him. "I don't remember the last time a man volunteered to do dishes around here. The Second Coming must be close at hand!"

Frank laughs and grabs a dish towel. He looks down at his feet. "I wanted a minute alone with you," he says. "To thank you for last night. I appreciate you understandin' about Liza."

I hand him a dripping plate. "I just want you to be happy. And now I'm the one who needs your help."

Frank dries the plate and reaches for another one. "Anything. I'll do anything you want."

I smirk. "Anything? Can I borrow your car tomorrow? I want to drive to Winston and see J.T."

Frank shakes his head. "I'm not sure that's such a good idea. You haven't had a lot of drivin' experience yet, and I worry about horseshoe nails on the road. You're almost sure to get a flat tire."

Finished with the dishes, I take the soapy rag and wash off the table. "The car would be quicker, but I'll get up early and hitch Patience to the wagon."

Frank crosses his arms. "Your pa would be worried sick about you travelin' alone. I'll let you drive the Model T, but I'm goin' with you."

I wink at Frank. "That's what I wanted all along, but I knew it would take you a while to see it my way."

Frank laughs. "God help J.T. You'll give that boy a run for his money."

Snow starts midmorning and doesn't let up. "We don't usually get snow for Christmas," Pa says. "It sure is pretty."

I lean my forehead against the windowpane. If this keeps up, there's no way Frank and I will be going to Winston tomorrow. "Think I'll sweep off the porch," I tell Pa. "I need some fresh air."

Using the broom, I knock snow off the swing and the rockers. Then I sweep the floor and steps.

"Jessie, Jessie!"

I look up from my sweeping and drop the broom. I take off across the yard and lose my footing on an icy patch. Scrambling to keep my balance, I yell, "J.T., J.T.!"

He trudges through the snow, and I tramp toward him. Finally we can touch each other. My hands tangle in his icy hair.

His arms circle my waist and he laughs. "Jessie, darlin', I'd like nothing better than to hold you all day, but my feet are frozen."

I can feel myself beaming, happiness shining around me like a halo.

"Step into my kitchen," I tell him, "and I'll fix your feet right up."

I place a pan of lukewarm soapy water on the kitchen floor. "Put your feet in."

J.T. eases his feet into the water and towels off his wet hair. "Earl and I had car trouble yesterday," he says. "That Model T hasn't been the same since Liza's mama drove it through the henhouse."

I bend down and kiss J.T.'s cheek. "I was waiting for you. Even had on a blue velveteen dress."

J.T. smiles. "I'm mighty sorry I missed seein' you in it. We slept in a barn last night, and soon as it was daylight walked the rest of the way home."

I hurry to Pa's room and bring back a pair of wool socks. "These will warm you up."

He puts them on and then pulls me down into his lap. He kisses me until I can't think straight, and then whispers, "Jessie, there's a present for you in my coat pocket."

I reach around to his coat, draped on the back of the chair. In the pocket I feel a small box. My fingers close around it. I wave the tiny package at J.T. "Is this for me?"

"Go ahead and open it," he says. "I wasn't here for your sixteenth birthday, so it's a birthday and Christmas present combined."

I untie the ribbon, tear the paper, and lift the lid. "Aah!" My breath catches from the beauty of it. "Oh, J.T., I love it! I've never had a piece of jewelry before." A heart with a pearl in the middle hangs from a gold chain.

"Let me fasten it for you," J.T. says. I move my braid to the side and he works the clasp. "Jessie Pearl is a beautiful girl," he whispers. "Someday she's gonna be my wife."

1924

33 | FORGET ME NOT

The dogwood trees are blooming outside my bedroom window. Their white blossoms are a sure sign that spring is here.

Tears threaten to spill over as I open my treasure box and see the snapshot of Anna and Carrie. When this picture was taken, they had no idea what troubles were ahead of them. Next I touch a lock of Ky's hair, and the red ribbon from J.T. My treasures remind me of the people I've made promises to: Carrie, Anna, Ky, and J.T. Finally I snatch the letter that's weighing on my mind. I put it in my overalls pocket and yell for Frank. "I'm taking the Model T for a spin."

Once outside, I pick some of the blue forget-me-nots from the flower garden. I make a small bouquet and tie it with tobacco twine. After placing the flowers on the passenger seat, I crank the car. Driving alone clears my head and gives me a feeling of freedom. Someday I'm gonna be a woman to be reckoned with, just like Maude.

Closing the throttle, I brake and stop the car in front of Stony Knoll Church. A gentle breeze ruffles my hair on the way to Carrie's grave. I kneel and touch the words carved on her tombstone: *For everything there is a season.*

"I brought you some forget-me-nots, Carrie." I place the flowers on her grave. "I have some things to tell you. Things I've been saving up for a long while. Though I didn't see it at the time, you were right to trust me with Ky, but there have been some rough patches. I lost him when I was doing the wash, and he cut his hand. After that I tried harder to keep him safe. Just so you know, I would die to protect him."

I reach into my pocket and wipe my face with a handkerchief. "Frank's had an awful time, crippled with loneliness. But now he's in love again—with Liza Phillips, of all people. I guess miracles really do happen, because she's turned into a woman I respect. I know you're wondering how that happened. It all started when Frank taught me to drive. She'll be a good mother for Ky, but it'll break my heart. I guess that's one problem you didn't see coming. How much it would hurt me to give him up."

My eyes feel like they've been scratched with sandpaper, but there's relief in telling the whole truth. "Carrie, it's been a year full of hurt. Anna took sick and went away to Asheville. It nearly killed us all, especially Cole. I don't know how it works after you die, but if you can, please help bring her home soon."

I open the top button of my shirt and touch my necklace. "I love J.T., love him with all my heart, but there's a whole big world out there and I've only seen a tiny piece of it."

Sobbing, I pull out the secret envelope. "See this letter? It's my acceptance to a school for teachers. Part of me wants to go away, and the other part can't stand the thought. How can I leave all the people I love most? Help me, Carrie. Help me decide."

I wrap my arms around the cool granite, and finally I hear her voice inside my head. *Jessie, follow your heart.*

I climb back into the Model T and drive to Anna's house. Maude is peeling potatoes when I charge in the back door.

"Lord, Jessie," she says, "what's wrong? You look worse than somethin' the cat dragged in."

I sit down at the kitchen table and cover my eyes with my hands. "I've been talking to Carrie."

Maude puts down her knife and takes a seat across from me. "If you're talkin' to the dead, you've got bigger problems than I can help you with."

I laugh in spite of myself. "Maude, I don't know what to do. Carrie told me to listen to my heart, but my heart's greedy. It wants two different things."

Maude reaches across the table and pats my hand. "When your heart doesn't know the answer, it's time to use your head."

34 | SAYING I DO

Spring gives way to early summer, and I'm no closer to making a decision.

"Jessie, Jessie girl," Frank says. "You're turnin' into a daydreamer. Did you hear a word I said?" He puts his arm around Liza on the parlor settee. "We're plannin' to get married two weeks from Sunday. Liza wants to be a June bride."

Pa leans forward in his chair, resting his arms on his thighs. "That's good news," he says. "I'm happy for both of you."

Ky cuddles against me in the rocking chair. He's only two years old. His memories will fade of the time I spent being his mother, but I will never forget any of it. Not his first steps, or the nights he had croup, or how sweet it sounds when he calls me Jay. "I'll get Frank's room ready," I say, "and pack away the rest of Carrie's things."

Liza looks down at her shoes and takes Frank's hand. "You don't have to do that," she says.

Frank pulls at his shirt collar as if it's too tight. "I don't know how to handle this," he says, "without causin' a world of hurt...but Liza and I can't live here."

I bend down and kiss Ky's cheek. "Why? Is it because Liza and I have had our differences?"

She shakes her head. "No, Jessie. It's because Frank lived here with Carrie. There are too many memories. We need to make a fresh start, and my father has offered to give us the land I was set to inherit."

Pa frowns, and the deep wrinkles on his face remind me of a dry creekbed. I'm not sure how he can run the farm without help. "Where will you be livin'?" he asks.

"With Liza's parents," Frank says. "At least until we can build a house." He looks Pa in the eyes. "J.T. doesn't like factory work. He hates bein' cooped up inside. I bet the two of you could strike a deal and work this farm together."

Pa purses his lips and nods. "That would solve all our problems, wouldn't it? And I know Jessie has missed that boy somethin' terrible."

I do miss J.T., and his coming back is the answer to a prayer. It's a sign that I belong at home.

Sunshine streams through the church windows. "Happy is the bride that the sun shines on," Maude whispers.

I hope that proves true. Most of our neighbors have turned out for the big day. After watching Frank grieve, everybody just wants him to be happy.

J.T. reaches over and squeezes my hand. "It's a shame Liza is marryin' Frank," he says. "I enjoyed all the sweets she made when she was tryin' to catch my eye."

I smother a giggle in my handkerchief. "Stop it. This is supposed to be a solemn occasion."

Frank waits for Liza in front of the pulpit. He looks handsome with his dark hair all slicked back, but a tad nervous too.

Abe and Bett Bowman rosin up their bows for the wedding march. J.T. and I rise to our feet, turning for our first glimpse of Liza. She glides down the aisle wearing her mother's white satin dress. Her father places her hand in Frank's.

"Dearly beloved," Preacher White begins, "we are gathered here today to witness the marriage of Frank Logan and Liza Phillips."

My eyes never leave Frank's face. He's finally happy and at peace.

When it's time for the vows, I think of Carrie. "Wilt thou love her, in sickness and in health, and forsaking all others keep thee only unto her, so long as ye both shall live?"

"I will," Frank answers.

Liza repeats her vows in a soft voice. She looks radiant.

Preacher White prays, asking God to bless their union. He turns to Frank. "You may kiss your bride!"

Abe and Bett play their fiddles as Frank and Liza stride up the aisle. J.T. puts his arm around me. "Why are you cryin'?" he asks.

After the wedding supper, J.T. and I settle into the front porch swing. Pa rocks close by with Ky in his arms. "I'm glad you're gonna be my partner," he says to J.T.

J.T. nods. "I can pay you for a couple of acres with the money I've saved up."

Pa shrugs and hands Ky one of his carved animals. "I ain't worried about the details," he says. "We'll get 'em worked out." Then he glances down at Ky. "This is his last night stayin' with us."

The tears in Pa's eyes tug at my heart. "It's not far to the Phillipses' farm," I say. "You can walk over and visit Ky most every day."

Pa taps his foot against the floorboard. "It won't be the same as him livin' here with us. The house will feel awful lonely again."

I lean my head back against the swing. Everybody has left home except for me. I'm all Pa has left.

35 | THE BALLAD OF JESSIE PEARL

It's been two weeks since Frank and Liza said their I do's. With a bandana I wipe the sweat off my forehead as I lean against my hoe. The tobacco field stretches out before me as far as I can see.

"It's a scorcher," J.T. says, working in the row beside me.

I grin and duck my head. So much for romance. My nose is sunburned and I smell like a polecat.

Pa moves just ahead of us in the row beside J.T. "Hurry it up," he says. "Maude will have pintos and hot cornbread waitin'."

I push the soil up around a leafy green plant and move on to the next one.

"What in tarnation is wrong with Cole?" Pa asks.

Cole hurries toward us with all the grace of a grizzly bear. He waves a piece of paper and yells, "Anna, Anna!" All three of us drop our hoes and run. Our brogans stir up a cloud of red dust.

Tears flow like a river down Cole's face. My heart beats double time. I reach for J.T.'s hand and squeeze it tight.

"She's comin' home," Cole says. "She's cured and comin' home!"

I launch myself at J.T., and he swings me around like a carousel at the county fair. Pa turns away, closing his eyes to pray. Cole throws the letter into the air and wraps his massive arms around Pa.

"Let him go," J.T. says with a laugh, "before you break a couple of his ribs!"

On the day of Anna's homecoming, the house smells of fried chicken and fresh baked biscuits. I've cleaned every room except Ky's nursery. I haven't opened the door since the day he left. I can't bear to.

Maude looks up from stirring the potatoes. "Jessie," she says, "it's about time to pull your cake out of the oven."

While I'm making the icing, Vivi tugs on my overalls. "Don't you want to look bootiful for Mama?"

I smile down at Vivi in her new dress. "You look beautiful

enough for both of us," I say. But that answer doesn't satisfy her.

"You should look bootiful," she says.

Maude nods her agreement. "Slap some icing on that cake," she says, "and then get yourself fixed up. Not many days are as special as this one."

I open the closet in Frank's room and take out Carrie's good spring dress—the one made of green cotton foulard, with a pleated skirt and side pockets. I slip into the dress and tug my hair free from its braid.

Fastening my necklace, I catch the reflection of Carrie's dulcimer in the mirror. I lift it from the bedside table and pluck the strings. I can almost hear her playing for Anna's homecoming.

I put the dulcimer back and take my acceptance letter from my overalls. Though I can't go to college, I think Anna will be proud of me when she reads it. I slip it into the dress's right pocket so I can show her.

"Jessie Pearl," Pa calls, "are you gonna primp all day?"

From the parlor doorway I watch Ky, Vivi, and Rose Lynn playing on the floor. Ky puts a squirrel into the ark Pa carved for his animals. "Not like that," Vivi bosses. "They go in two by two."

Pa, Tom, and J.T. stand near the window, hoping to catch the first glimpse of Cole's Model T. "Where's Sophie?" I ask.

Tom turns around and whistles. "She's in the kitchen with Maude. Jessie Pearl, you clean up right nice."

J.T. points to my necklace and smiles.

Frank rises from the settee when he sees me. "Jessie, could I talk to you out on the porch?"

I shrug and follow him outside. "What's wrong?"

He hands me a slip of paper with Carrie's handwriting on it. "She asked me to give you this," he says. "She knew that whenever I remarried, you'd be free."

I scan the words scribbled on the paper—"The Ballad of Jessie Pearl."

Jessie Pearl is a beautiful girl
She's a beautiful girl, that Jessie Pearl
Jessie Pearl, oh, Jessie Pearl
She's a beautiful girl, that Jessie Pearl.

She lost her ma and her sister's ill
A graveyard waits upon the hill
She lost her ma and her sister's ill
That Jessie Pearl is a grieving girl.

Jessie has a choice to make
Wondering 'bout which road to take
Jessie has a choice to make
Will Jessie Pearl be a lonely girl?

At the bottom of the paper Carrie had scrawled, *Write the last verse for me, Jessie. It's up to you.*

"What is she trying to tell me?" I ask.

Frank shakes his head. "I can't say for sure, but she wondered if you'd be a farm wife like your ma or go away to college."

I sink down on the porch swing. "I need to be by myself. I have to think things through."

Lost in thought, I barely notice when J.T. sits down beside me. He reaches up and touches my hair. "Talk to me, Jessie."

With trembling hands, I reach into my pocket and hand him the letter. "I applied when you were in Winston."

J.T. scowls while he reads it, but before he can say what's on his mind, Cole's Model T rumbles to a stop. I jump to my feet. "Anna's home!" I cry.

My family spills onto the porch, everybody laughing and talking at the same time.

Vivi pushes past Pa, running as fast as her short legs will carry her. "Mama!" she yells. "Mama!"

Cole has just helped Anna from the car. He bends down and swoops Vivi into his arms. Anna launches herself at both of them, clinging like moss to a tree. I drink in the sight of her. My sister is absolutely beautiful.

"Anna, today you're the guest of honor," Maude says. "Just sit and visit. Liza is watching the children, and Sophie and Jessie can help me finish up the meal."

Anna takes a seat and strokes the kitchen table's smooth oak top.

"I can hardly believe I'm here," she says. "I've been so homesick. It's hard to be away from the people you love."

I fill the water pitcher with shaky hands. The people I love are right here.

Sophie mashes the potatoes and adds some milk. "There's no place like home," she says. "I would never argue with that. But there's something to be said for seeing the world beyond this community. I enjoyed the time I spent teaching."

Maude pours gravy from the skillet into a bowl. "You can always fall back on teachin'," she says. "A woman needs to be able to support herself. I've had to do it for many a year." She opens the warming oven and does a final check. "Jessie, we're havin' a feast! Call this crowd to dinner."

We gather around the table, linking hands in a family circle. "Dear Lord," Pa prays. "Words can hardly express how grateful we feel today. Thank you for bringin' Anna back home to us. Bless this family and the fine meal we're about to eat. Amen."

"Amen," we all murmur.

I pass the potatoes to J.T., but he barely takes a spoonful. "Anna," he says, "tell us about the mountains. I've never seen 'em."

"They're full of beauty," she says. "Especially in the fall. It's different from around here. Our leaves don't hold nearly as much color. I'll miss those mountains," she says. "I surely will."

Anna's homecoming should be full of joy, but the look on J.T.'s face hurts my heart.

"Everybody out of the kitchen," Maude says. "It won't take me but a minute to wash the dishes. All of you should spend some time with Anna."

"I'll help you," Sophie says. "That way the work will go faster and we can all visit afterward."

Maude fixes her with a steely stare. "I said I'd do it myself."

I wait until everybody is settled in the parlor and slip back to the kitchen. Maude stands against the kitchen sink with her back to me. Her shoulders heave, and she pulls a handkerchief out of her apron pocket.

I walk across the kitchen and slip my arms around Maude's waist. "Tell me your troubles," I say.

Maude wipes her eyes and blows her nose. "With Anna back home, it's time for me to go."

I rest my head against her back. "Are you worried about money?"

Maude snorts. "Lord no, child. I ain't spent a penny of what Cole has been payin' me. I just like feelin' needed."

I dry the pots and pans for Maude in silence. I'm afraid if I say another word, she'll order me out of the kitchen.

"Don't you tell anybody I was cryin'," she says, "or I'll switch you with a hickory stick."

I smile at her. "Don't worry. You're so tough nobody would believe it."

When the back door slams behind J.T., I know he is headed for the fishing shack. "Excuse me, Maude. I have to talk to J.T."

She peers into my eyes. "He's a fine boy, Jessie Pearl. If I was younger, I'd give you a run for your money."

When I step inside the fishing shack, J.T. pulls my letter from his pocket. "Why did you keep this a secret from me?"

I scrub at the tears threatening to fall. "Because it's just a dream. I've had to grow up and let it go."

J.T. pulls me into his arms and clutches my shoulders. He kisses away the tears spilling onto my cheeks, and then he kisses my throat where his necklace falls. He hugs me tighter, burying his face in my hair. "I hate the thought of you leavin' me," he says.

I close my eyes and push myself against him as tight as two peas in a pod. "The only place I'm going is to the tobacco field, and you'll be in the row beside me."

J.T. looks down into my eyes. "Maybe someday, Jessie, but not yet. If I hadn't gone away for a while, I would never have been satisfied here. I'm thinkin' the same is true for you."

I rest my cheek against his chest. "It would break my heart to go. I don't think I can leave you, or my pa either."

He reaches into his pocket and hands me a handkerchief. "Girl, you are soakin' my shirt through with your tears."

I mop my face with it and look up at him. "Would you wait for me?"

J.T. shakes his head and gives me a sad smile. "No promises, Jessie. That wouldn't be fair to either of us."

I stand on my tiptoes and kiss his lips. "Even if I went away to college, my heart would still belong to you."

J.T. crushes me against his chest. "Ah, Jessie, it don't work that way. Once you're out in the big world, anything can happen."

When darkness falls, I slip into Frank's room and strum Carrie's dulcimer. I close my eyes and sing the ballad that she wrote for me. Then I take a pencil and scribble the last verse:

Jessie's life is changin' fast
She's in love, but will it last?
Jessie's life is changin' fast
Should Jessie Pearl be a traveling girl?

36 | HEADED FOR THE BLUE RIDGE

After the last tobacco stalk has been stripped bare, it's time for me to leave home. Most of the neighbors have gathered in our yard to say their goodbyes to me.

Viney gives me a bag of peppermints for the trip. "Don't forget to write," she says.

Of course Pansy Pilcher has to get her two cents in. "You'd be better off to keep your tail at home and give J.T. a passel of young'uns," she says.

I look over her shoulder and point to the biggest oak in our yard. "Billy just pushed Bobby out of the tree. Looks to me like a fight is brewing."

Pansy hurries off to keep her boys from killing each other. Maude laughs. "I guess that shut her up," she says. Maude is going to stay on and look after Pa. She hugs me and then pulls her handkerchief from her pocket. "Must be something in the air."

I reach up and kiss her cheek. "I love you, Maude."

"Ah, go on with you," she says, but I'll never forget all she's done for me, even lending me the money for school.

Holding Rose Lynn, Sophie tells me that she's proud of me. "I know it's hard to leave," she says, "but I don't think you'll ever regret this decision."

"I don't know what I'll do without my baby sister," Tom says. "Come home every chance you get."

Frank catches me in a hug. "Jessie," he says, "you're the best sister-in-law that ever was."

"Look after Ky," I whisper, "and take Patches home with you. He loves Ky more than me anyway."

Liza steps up, breaking the hug between Frank and me. "We've had our battles, but I want only the best for you," she says.

I look her straight in the eyes. "Same here. You make Frank and Ky happy. That carries a lot of weight with me."

Anna takes both my hands in hers. "Ma would be so proud," she says, "and Carrie too. Take care of yourself, Jessie."

A sob catches in my throat, and Cole claps me on the back. "Don't get Anna started," he says, "or you'll never get on the road."

I bend down and hug Ky with one arm and Vivi with the other. Patches barks from all the excitement, and Ky and Vivi run to play with him. My heart aches, but it pounds with excitement too.

Pa has waited until last and crushes me to his chest. "Baby girl," he says, "don't ever forget where you came from."

I hug him back for all I'm worth. "There's no chance of that, Pa. No chance at all. I've got deep roots."

J.T. takes my hand and pulls me away from all the people that I love best in the world. He swings my bags into the back of Frank's Model T. "Dry your tears, Jessie Pearl. We're headed for the Blue Ridge!"

AUTHOR'S NOTE

In 2008, my son, Alex, was given an assignment in his eighth-grade history class to interview relatives and record their stories. Alex talked to my mother, who told him that one of his great-grandmother's sisters, Crawley Wooten, had died when she was only twenty years old. Crawley left behind a ten-month-old baby, Junior, and a letter planning her own funeral. When my mother was growing up, she often read the letter.

Alex wondered what happened to Junior. He found out that his great-grandmother, Lena, was his age, fourteen, at the time of Crawley's death. She stepped in and became Junior's mother until his father later remarried. Alex couldn't imagine handling that much responsibility as a teenager. Alex also wondered what disease had killed Crawley. A distant cousin told him it was tuberculosis. Because the disease is contagious, the family worried that Junior would get sick too, but he never did.

This family story called to me as a writer and wouldn't let go. I decided to write a novel inspired by actual events. I began reading novels set in the early 1920s, North Carolina history books, memoirs written from sanatoriums, and doctors' accounts of the disease. I consulted experts at the North Carolina Museum of History and the Swannanoa Valley Museum.

I learned that tuberculosis was the leading cause of death in the United States during the 1800s and well into the next century. Many people called the disease "consumption," because it seemed to consume its victims, causing severe weight loss and a ghostly pale complexion. Other symptoms included a hacking cough, blood-tinged phlegm, joint pain, diarrhea, and swollen legs.

Research by Robert Koch proved in 1882 that tuberculosis is contagious—spread from person to person through the air when infected people cough and spit. In 1885 Dr. Edward Livingston Trudeau established a special hospital to isolate infected people.

Located at Saranac Lake in New York's Adirondack Mountains, this sanatorium became the model for other tuberculosis hospitals in the United States. By 1925, there were more than five hundred sanatoriums with almost seven hundred thousand beds. In a sanatorium, patients were treated with good food, plenty of rest, and fresh air. Many even slept outside on covered porches.

Though Saranac Lake is more famous, The Villa in Asheville, North Carolina, preceded it by several years. The Villa was established by Dr. Horatio Page Gatchell, who considered Asheville's fresh mountain air optimal for treating lung disease. Asheville attracted so many sufferers that a pamphlet published in 1915 by the U.S. Public Health Service declared North Carolina to have the largest number of tuberculosis patients in the world.

Medicine to treat tuberculosis was not readily available until after the end of World War II. As the number of cures gradually increased, sanatoriums were closed down. In 1954, *Life* magazine reported that the last patient had been released from Saranac Lake. In the United States today, only one freestanding sanatorium—in Lantana, Florida—remains.

My deepest thanks to the people who made my writing dream a reality: my mother, Carolyn Williams, the keeper of family stories and traditions; Mike Fowler, history teacher at Tampa Preparatory School, whose creative history project sent us digging for family stories; my husband, David, whose encouragement kept me from giving up; Mary Grey James, formerly of East/West Literary, and Deborah Warren, who now represents me; Cynthia Chapman Willis, my best writing buddy; Susan Kaye Riley, for cheering the loudest; Joyce Sweeney, teacher, mentor, and friend; Jeannine Q. Norris, Eileen Goldenberg, Joni Klein-Higger, Sarah Bridgeton, and Diana Sharp, my first readers; Kent Brown, Carolyn Yoder, and the staff at the Highlights Foundation; and my editor, Stephen Roxburgh, and the staff at namelos.

CPSIA information can be obtained at www.ICGtesting.com
Printed in the USA
BVOW07*1119180913

331330BV00001B/4/P

9 781608 981410